ATLAS
AND THE MULTIVERSE

ATLAS

AND THE MULTIVERSE

SEEKING COURAGE

**CHANDON
SIMAN**

For my children, Atlas and Lilou,
who inspired the characters of the story.

To my wife, Kiala,
who supported me every step of the way.

A special thanks to my friend,
Jill Jordan, and my sister Sireenah Michlovich,
for helping me find my voice.

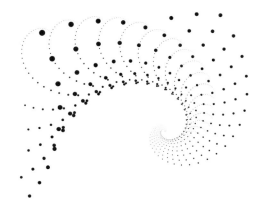

Chapter 1

Atlas, Lilou, and Nico stood outside their new home in the North End of Boise, Idaho, waiting for the bus to arrive to take them to their first day of middle school.

"Can someone please explain to me why Mom moved us back to Idaho a week before school started?" Lilou whined. "I miss the beaches, the sunsets, and the city. I don't know if you two remember, but there's nothing here but mountains, rivers, and potatoes."

"Of course, everyone knows Idaho is famous for its potatoes. But fun fact, Idaho is also a leading producer of lentils," Nico said.

Lilou rolled her eyes. "Wow ... you really need to use the word *fun* a bit more sparingly. For someone who prides himself on his enormous vocabulary, I don't think I've ever heard you use that word correctly."

"You know exactly why Adora brought us back here, Lilou," Atlas reminded her. "Or maybe you don't remember the three of us getting bullied all those years."

Atlas was the most recent addition to the household. He had short, light brown hair and honey-colored skin. He'd grown up an orphan. Never knowing who his biological parents were, he had spent most of his early childhood moving from foster home to foster home. This made it difficult to make any real friends.

It was Adora, a middle-aged, caring woman who had adopted Atlas at the age of eight from his dysfunctional foster home. By that time, Adora had adopted Lilou and Nico, both the same age as Atlas.

Soon after she adopted Atlas, she moved all three kids to San Diego, California. Over the years, the three of them had to find ways of getting along, which they did for the most part, although mostly because all three had a difficult time making friends outside of each other.

"Umm ... I kinda remember the two of you getting bullied, but I was perfectly fine with being alone — ever heard of an independent woman?" Lilou replied. "Also, that's not the real reason we moved back here. That's just what Mom told you. We moved because she was trying to get away from Alex, that hideous abusive boyfriend of hers — the one who put those bruises on her arm."

"Well, I'm glad Adora never forced us to meet him, unlike her past boyfriends," Atlas said.

The bus arrived. The kids hopped on and took the seats closest to the driver, knowing it was probably their best chance of being ignored.

"I know it's hard for you, but try to keep your head down, Atlas. I don't want to attract any unwanted attention this early in the morning," Lilou said.

Like most kids, Atlas, at age twelve, was nervous for his first day of seventh grade. But Atlas felt he had more to be worried about than other middle schoolers. Atlas was already quite tall for his age. This past summer, he'd grown another two full inches, and now stood nearly six feet tall. Back at his old school in California, Atlas had been bullied by his peers, who often called him names like Oaf, Beanstalk, and his least favorite of all, Slenderman.

Before the bus had a chance to take off, a boy at the back wearing a black hoodie and a red trucker hat stood and shouted, "Hey, Stretch! I think you got on the wrong bus. The bus to the high school is on the other side of the street."

So much for keeping my head down, Atlas thought, slouching in his seat.

"Maybe he was talking to someone else," Nico said, glancing back to see if the boy was looking at them.

"Do you see another person on this bus that looks like they should be in high school, Nico?" Atlas replied, looking to his sister for help.

Lilou shook her head in disappointment. She was a strong-minded young girl with caramel-colored skin, big brown eyes, and long dark hair. You could call her a Type A, which was a polite way of saying she was bossy. Knowing Atlas would not stand up for himself, she stood, faced the back of the bus, and smiled. "Hey! You, there. You're kinda cute. Do you mind if I come back there and sit with you?"

The boy in the hoodie, taken aback by Lilou's question, had a hard time finding his next words. "R-R-Really? You think so? Su-r-r-e, you can sit with me," he stuttered out.

"Oh ... I'm sorry. I wasn't talking to you. I was talking to that cute boy in the row in front of you," Lilou returned with a self-satisfied smile.

The boy tilted his head and took a long hard look at the short, pudgy boy she had called *cute*. He wondered if he'd been mistaken, before noticing all eyes were on him. "Yeah ... sure ... whatever," he scoffed. He sat and pulled out his phone in an attempt to dismiss the awkward exchange.

The pudgy boy, who looked like he belonged in elementary school, blushed, then grinned from ear to ear as he scooted over to make room for Lilou.

Lilou, with no intention of moving to the back of the bus, sat and turned to her brothers. "You know, the best part about being a girl in middle school is, if you ever need to make a boy feel uncomfortable, all you have to do is talk to him."

The short bus ride ended with no further interruptions, and the siblings got off and checked their schedules.

"Hmm ... it looks like we only got Science class together," Lilou said. "And that's not until the end of the day. I guess I'll be seeing you two later." She turned and confidently walked off to class.

"What do you have first, Nico?" Atlas asked.

"Algebra 2 Honors. It's an advanced math class. I suppose I'll be with all eighth graders," Nico answered, gazing at a group of eighth graders in the distance who were pushing around one of the new, smaller seventh graders.

Atlas had to deal with being gawkily tall for his age; Nico had his own set of challenges. He was short in stature, with olive-toned skin and jet-black hair that was always neatly combed to one side. He was also something of a wonderchild, highly intelligent, and a bit of an oddball, which made it difficult for him to relate to his peers.

"Don't worry, Nico. Keep your head down and focus on your schoolwork, and you'll be fine," Atlas said. He patted his brother on the back before walking to class.

Although this was his first day of middle school, Atlas was no stranger to first days. As an orphan, he'd been forced to move around a lot and had learned long ago that the best way to get through school was to keep his head down and keep to himself. Sticking to his plan, the rest of his morning went reasonably smoothly.

A few kids randomly approached him to ask him how tall he was, and only one of his teachers joked about Atlas being taller than him. He saw the boy from the bus only one other time in the hallway. Atlas ducked behind a locker in time to avoid another confrontation. After the lunch bell rang, he entered the cafeteria and searched for his brother and sister. Atlas didn't see Lilou, but he spotted Nico sitting alone at a table in the back and joined him.

"Hey, how was algebra?" Atlas said.

"Great. They're moving me into precalculus. But they said I'd have to take it online because they don't offer it here," Nico answered, looking relieved.

"That's great. I guess you won't be stuck with all the eighth graders after all," Atlas said with a smile.

Lilou took her seat across from her brothers. "I had forgotten how different kids are here. They talk differently, act differently, and dress differently. They aren't obsessed with their looks or the latest social media trends, like the kids we went to school with back in California. I think I'm happy to be back. How're your days going?"

"So far, so good. I was telling Atlas that they're moving me into precalculus," Nico said proudly.

"Good for you, Nico," Lilou replied. She turned to Atlas. "Well ... what about you?"

"Okay, I guess. I saw that boy from the bus in the hall, though," he said, glancing around to make sure the boy wasn't nearby.

"Oh, him. Don't worry about him. His name's Zach. I heard he got expelled from his last two schools. I imagine he won't be around for long," Lilou said.

"Well, that would be a relief. So, what class do you guys have nex ... ahhh!" A sharp pain hit Atlas in the back of his head, causing him to bellow.

Lilou checked to make sure nobody was paying attention, then whispered, "Is that another one of your migraines?"

"Yeah, and they're getting worse," Atlas replied, holding his throbbing head.

"You really need to get that taken care of," Nico said.

Yeah, thanks, Atlas thought.

The migraines had started a few months earlier. Adora had taken him to see several doctors over the summer break, but none could help him. One suggested the migraines could be caused by his childhood trauma, but Atlas never accepted that idea.

His head still pounding, Atlas dragged himself to his afternoon classes. He spent most of the afternoon with his head down on desks. He had one class left; luckily, Lilou and Nico would both be there. He hoped it wouldn't be too bad.

Entering Period 6 Science, Atlas scanned the room for them. He spotted Nico by the door and gave him a slight wave. Lilou was sitting in the back. He walked over to take the open seat next to her when a familiar voice taunted him. "Hey, Stretch! How's the weather up there?" the boy from the bus sneered. *Great, him again.* Realizing he'd have to pass the boy on his way to the back, Atlas cut his losses and took the closest seat he could find.

Once the class settled, the teacher gave a boring talk about his classroom rules and procedures and what the students could expect to learn that year. Throughout the lecture, Atlas could hear the boy from the bus giggling with a friend behind him. Atlas assumed the laughter was directed at him. Then, without warning, his migraine got worse, accompanied by a piercing sound in his ears. Atlas grabbed the back of his head and struggled to stay in his seat as the shrill sound grew louder and louder, until finally, everything fell silent.

Atlas, can you hear me?

It was the voice of a stranger, and it sounded like it was coming from inside his head. The voice repeated itself: *Can you hear me?* Then it stopped. Atlas jumped out of his seat. "Who said that?" he exclaimed, drawing the unwanted attention of every kid in the class.

Atlas stood frozen, with blurred vision and sweat dripping down his forehead, until the silence gave way to the normal sounds of the classroom. His eyes regained focus. Out of the corner of his eye, he saw the teacher waving, trying to get his attention.

"Youngman, is there something wrong?" the teacher asked.

"Bathroom!"

"Okay, the pass is right here." The teacher held it up.

"Thank you," Atlas said, only half paying attention as he searched for a clue to the source of the voice. As he pivoted around, he caught sight of his sister.

Lilou, who was half-covering her face with her hand to hide her mingled expression of concern and embarrassment, mouthed, "Take the pass."

Atlas turned back toward the teacher, who was still holding the bathroom pass, waiting for Atlas to take it.

"Right," Atlas whispered to himself, wiping the sweat off his forehead with his sleeve. He slowly walked to the front of the room. As he reached for the pass, he stumbled and fell to the floor as his long leg caught on a desk. Without looking to see the expression on everyone's faces, he got to his feet, grabbed the pass, and ran for the door.

Lilou took a deep breath, stood, and took center stage, realizing she'd once again have to speak on behalf of her brother. "Sorry about that, my brother has a uh ... condition ... stomach condition," she explained in a poor attempt at damage control. "I think I'd better go check on him." She looked across the room at her brother. "Nico, do you want to come?"

"Do the three of you normally go to the bathroom together?" the teacher said, looking confused.

"Yes. I mean no! Well, sometimes," Lilou said with a crooked smile. She hurried to the front, grabbed Nico's hand, and pulled him out the door.

"I don't think that teacher is fond of us," Nico said, trying to keep up with Lilou as she ran down the hall.

"Oh, who cares? Let's just find Atlas. What was that about, anyway?"

Nico shrugged his shoulders.

At the boy's bathroom, Lilou surveyed the hall to make sure no boys were coming, then barged in. "Atlas, are you in here?"

"Lilou, is that you?" Atlas asked from inside a stall.

"Were you expecting another girl to meet you in the bathroom?"

Atlas came out of the stall. "Was everybody laughing at me?" he asked, more worried about what his peers would think of him when he returned to class than about the voice in his head.

Lilou shot Atlas a concerned look. "Who cares? Can you please explain what that was about? Why did you shout, 'Who said that?' in the middle of class?"

"I can't explain it. My migraine got worse. I heard a buzzing noise I'd never heard before — it was so loud. Then everything went silent, and out of nowhere, I heard a voice, except it sounded like it was inside my head."

"What did it say?" Nico asked.

Atlas, embarrassed, reluctantly answered. "It said, 'Atlas, can you hear me?'"

"That's it? That could have literally been anyone in that classroom," Lilou said, disappointed.

"No, it wasn't like that. The voice really was in my head," Atlas repeated.

Lilou and Nico looked confused.

"Can we please just go home before the bell rings?" Atlas said, his shoulders slumping. "I don't want any one to see me."

Lilou brightened. "Now *that* I can get behind. Let's get out of here."

The siblings walked home to avoid another confrontation on the bus, especially after Atlas's outburst in class. It was a straight shot home, just ten blocks away. They were almost there when Lilou broke the silence.

She looked at Atlas intently. "Can we go over this again? What exactly did this *voice* say to you?"

"What does it matter? You don't believe me, anyway."

"I just want to have my story straight when the crazy police come and take my brother away is all," she said.

"You know, migraines have been known to cause hallucinations," Nico put in. "The spike in electrical waves moving across your auditory cortex could ..."

"Nico, please stop. School's out. We don't need a lecture," Lilou interrupted.

"I wasn't hallucinating. I heard a voice in my head," Atlas said petulantly, upset that they didn't believe him. He ran into the house just ahead of them.

"You're home. How was your first day of school in Idaho?" Adora shouted from down the hall, smiling. Adora had a youthful face; she was slim and athletic and had long and wavy, dark-chocolate-colored hair. Atlas ignored her and ran upstairs to his bedroom.

A minute later, Lilou and Nico barged through the front door.

Adora tried again: "Hey kids, how was your first day?"

"Oh, just terrific, great school. Idaho is just so beautiful in the fall," Lilou responded, as she and Nico dashed up the stairs.

"I'm never going back to that school," Atlas said when they burst into his and Nico's room. "Between being bullied again and hearing that voice, I've had enough."

"You're not going back? What about me?" Lilou demanded. "I'm the one who stood in the middle of class and said my brother has stomach problems. You have more explaining to do."

"I told you. It was a voice. I can't explain it, and I don't know where it came from," Atlas repeated in frustration.

"Well, forgive me if I'm a little skeptical," Lilou parried. "I hope for your sake and mine that everyone forgets your little performance today."

"I find that highly unlikely," Nico said. "I'm positive nothing more exciting happened at school today."

Lilou rolled her eyes. "Really?"

"What?" Nico shrugged, looking legitimately confused.

Atlas put his face in his hands. "As Nico said, it was probably just a migraine. Maybe I didn't hear anything at all. Can this day please just be over?"

That night, Atlas sat in bed across from Nico, who was asleep in his, and reflected on the events of the day. Over the years, he'd had many rough days at school, but this was by far the worst — and certainly the strangest. He thought about what that one doctor had said about his childhood trauma and started to wonder if he was right.

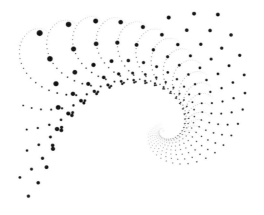

Chapter 2

A *tlas, my dear child, wake up.*

Atlas awoke in a cold sweat, sat, and surveyed the room. It was early morning, but the room was still dark, and it took a moment for his eyes to adjust. *What's happening to me?* he thought. He looked over at Nico's bed to see if the voice had been Nico's, but his brother was fast asleep. Atlas crawled out of his covers and scrambled to Nico's bedside.

"Nico," Atlas whispered. He shook the bed frame. "Nico, wake up."

Nico slowly opened his eyes. "What is it?"

"I heard it again."

"Heard what?"

"The voice."

Nico sat up sluggishly. "The voice? Oh, right. What did it say?"

"It said, *'Atlas, my dear child, wake up.'*"

"Hmm, that's interesting ..."

"What's interesting? What do you mean?"

"Well, last time it didn't call you its *dear child.*"

"Yeah ... so?" Atlas said.

"Was the voice male or female?"

"Who cares," Atlas said dismissively. "Why is it in my head?"

"Well?"

"Fine, it was a man's voice. Happy?"

"It seems to me that if the voice referred to you as their child, and the voice was male, then the voice must be your father's," Nico concluded.

"Very funny, Nico. I don't have a father, and even if I did, why would his voice be in my head?"

Atlas went over to his bed and threw himself on it.

"I don't think there's actually a voice inside your head," Nico said. "You were probably dreaming, or the migraines are causing you to hallucinate again."

16

"Nico, I'm not hallucinating. I heard it ... I mean, I didn't hear it, because it was in my head." Atlas pointed to his temple, annoyed that Nico still didn't understand.

"It told you to wake up, and you're awake. So, now what?" Nico asked.

"How am I supposed to know? Nico, can you please go wake up Lilou?" Atlas prayed Nico would say yes.

"No way. You know how she is in the morning."

"Ugh, fine. I'll do it, but you're coming with me."

The boys tiptoed across the hall to Lilou's room and stood by her bed. "Lilou, wake up," Atlas whispered loudly, to no effect. He glanced at Nico, who shrugged. Atlas tried again. "Lilou, please wake up!" This time he rocked her shoulder back and forth.

Lilou rolled over and faced Atlas. "What do you want?" she mumbled; her eyes sealed shut.

Atlas, unsure if she'd heard him or was talking in her sleep, replied, "The voice, I heard it again."

Lilou half-opened her eyes. "Well, unless that voice told you that school is canceled for the rest of the year, I'm going back to sleep." She flipped back over and pulled her covers over her head.

"No, it said, '*Atlas, my dear child, wake up.*'"

Lilou reluctantly sat up in bed and rubbed her eyes. "*Dear child?*" she mumbled, shaking her head. "Who talks like that?" She seemed annoyed by the voice inside Atlas's head.

"Lilou, please, I ... Ahhh!" Atlas screamed as another stabbing pain hit him. He fell to the floor, holding his head, desperately trying to suppress another scream.

"Are you okay? Nico, get Mom!" Lilou ordered. "His migraines are getting worse." She placed an arm around Atlas's shoulder. "Nico, what are you waiting for?"

"Guys ... Are you seeing this?" Nico whispered.

Atlas looked in time to see a bright light emanating from the center of the room. It hovered a few feet above the ground. The light expanded until it formed a perfect circle. The circle shimmered with an array of iridescent colors, like the surface of an opalescent pearl. Behind the light, Atlas could just make out what appeared to be a silhouette of a man.

Then the man spoke.

Atlas, my child, you must find me before it is too late. Find Dr. Faraday! He will have the answers you seek!

Without warning, the circle vanished as fast as it had come.

"What the heck was that?" Lilou blurted out.

"And who was that" Atlas added, shocked.

"Okay, that's it, I'm getting Mom," Lilou announced, heading for the door.

"No, wait — that voice, that's the voice I've been telling you about," Atlas pleaded. He jumped in front of Lilou to keep her from leaving.

"That was no voice. That was a creepy man standing in my bedroom." Lilou pointed to where they'd seen the man's silhouette.

Nico started feeling the air as if trying to find something that would reveal itself. "It looked like some sort of portal ..."

Lilou crossed her arms. "A portal? What's a portal? Better yet, what's it doing in my room?"

"From what I've read, a portal is a doorway to a wormhole," Nico said.

"Okay ... Now, what's a wormhole?"

"A wormhole is like a highway between two points in spacetime," Nico said. "The other side of that wormhole could be ... well, anywhere."

"Great, that's helpful."

Atlas, whose head was still pounding, sat on the edge of Lilou's bed. "Nico, you said the voice could have been my father's. Did you mean that?"

"I can't say for certain, but I've found that the most obvious answer is often the right one," Nico replied.

"What did he mean by 'before it is too late' And who is Dr. Faraday?" Atlas said.

"You're not actually considering listening to that stranger, are you?" Lilou asked.

Although Atlas had often doubted himself in the past, now he was determined to solve this mystery. "What time is it?" he asked, frantically looking around for a clock.

"It's six-thirty. We need to get ready for school," Nico reminded them.

"I'm not going to school, Nico," Atlas retorted.

"Is it because of what happened yesterday?"

Atlas glared at his brother. "No, it's because of what happened one minute ago in this room. If that man was my father and he's in danger, I need to find him."

"Atlas, you don't know if that was your father," Lilou said. "And even if it was, what makes you so set on finding him?"

Atlas glared at her. "Hey, you *had* a father. You knew him. I never met either of my parents, remember? I have to try." He turned away in frustration.

Lilou paused. "You're right," she said. "I knew my father, but I wish I hadn't. My real parents were addicts, and I'm thankful I don't live with them any more. There's a reason parents give their kids up for adoption, remember?"

Atlas sat, feeling bad for bringing up Lilou's past. "I'm sorry. All I know about my parents is that my mother died giving birth to me, and I was never told anything about my father." He paused. "I didn't tell this, but over summer break, I asked Adora if I could search for my father. She said I wasn't ready. I listened because I didn't know where to start, but now I have something. As strange as it is, it's *something.*"

"Okay, let's say for a second that it was your father we saw. How do you expect to find this Dr. Faraday, anyway?" Lilou asked.

That can't be a common name, Atlas thought. He grabbed Lilou's laptop off her desk and started running a search for "Dr. Faraday."

"What are you doing?" she said.

"I'm looking for Dr. Faraday." To Atlas's surprise, there were a lot of Dr. Faradays. He found a few dentists, chiropractors, and even a therapist. "How am I supposed to narrow this down?" he said aloud.

"Here, move over. Let me try," Nico said.

"We need to hurry. It's almost time to leave for school," Atlas reminded him. "Adora is going to wonder what we're doing up here."

"Just give me a second," Nico said. "Okay, look, there's a professor of art history at Boise State University named Dr. Faraday. I have no idea if this is the one, but it's the only Dr. Faraday in Boise. You might as well start there. The campus is only ten minutes away."

"Listen, when it's time to get on the bus, you two distract Adora, and I'll grab my bike and head to the campus," Atlas said.

Nico nodded. "I can do that."

"No, that's not okay," Lilou said. "You're going to skip school and go looking for this stranger on your own? Look, I don't know what's going on with you or understand what we just saw, but if you really want to do this, we're coming with you." She walked over to the door. "I'll go downstairs and tell Mom we're riding our bikes to school today. It's only a few blocks away, and it's not an outrageous lie. She'll never suspect a thing."

Atlas placed his hand on the door handle to stop her. "No, wait. We don't need to lie. I'll go downstairs and tell Adora everything. She'll understand."

"*We* are going to go downstairs to tell Mom," Lilou corrected him.

Adora was preparing breakfast in the kitchen. "Hey, you guys are up. Are you excited about your second day of school?" she exclaimed.

"Mom, there's something I need to tell you. Can we sit down and talk?" Atlas said.

"Of course. We can talk about anything," Adora replied, looking puzzled. She stacked the last pancake on⌐ ⌐ plate and followed them into the dining room.

⌐ v were seated at the dining room table, Atlas

⌐n, remember how over the summer I told

⌐ly to look for my father?"

"I remember. Does this have something to do with that?"

"Well, yeah, sort of. I can't explain everything right now. You'll have to trust me, but it can't wait any longer." Atlas paused, realizing he hadn't had the time to think through his explanation. "We found this professor ... Dr. Faraday, he ..." Atlas hesitated as he struggled to finish the lie he'd started.

He looked at his brother and sister, who looked back with blank expressions. He remembered that he'd been planning to ask for an Ancestry test kit for his next birthday, which was just a month away. "... he studies genealogy and family heritage," Atlas continued. "He told us he could do a DNA test and compare the results with the database and see if anything matches," he finished in a strong voice.

Adora scanned the table to see which child would speak next and realized that all of them were looking to her to answer.

She said, "I always knew that someday I'd need to let you make this decision, Atlas. I just wasn't expecting it to be on the second day of middle school. Look, I know things haven't been easy, and I know I haven't been the best ..."

Lilou broke in. "Mom, you're ..."

"No, let me finish. I'm sorry I haven't been the best at finding ... well, a male companion. I thought Alex would be the one and be a father figure for this family someday, but that didn't work out as I'd hoped." Adora took a deep breath, holding back tears. "Wait right here. I need to grab something," she said, and walked upstairs.

"What do you think she's going to get?" Atlas asked.

"I have no idea," Lilou replied, her expression detached.

A minute later, Adora came back holding a shoebox. "Atlas, you know that your mother died during childbirth," she said. "What you don't know is that the hospital could never identify her body. They never found relatives or anyone that knew her. To this day, nobody has reported her missing. This also means there was no one to pass on her personal belongings to. She didn't have much, only what she had on her when she arrived at the hospital. I received it when I adopted you.

"I was going to give it to you on your thirteenth birthday, but I think today might be more appropriate. There isn't much in this box, but what is in it now belongs to you. I promise, after school, when you get home, I'll help you schedule an appointment with Dr. Faraday if that's what you want." Adora left the box in the middle of the table, stood, and walked back upstairs.

Atlas, realizing he might have left out a crucial detail about their plans for today, stared at the box.

"Well, aren't you going to open it?" Lilou asked, hinting with her eyes.

Atlas reached out and pulled the box in front of him. It was an ordinary shoebox, one that probably belonged to Adora. Atlas opened the lid. Inside were three items. He reached in and took out the first one.

"It's a photograph. But it's been torn," he said. The photo was of a man standing in the middle of a city street. Vehicles, which appeared to be floating, could be seen in the distance. There was also an array of neon signs, which seemed to be suspended high above the city sidewalks.

The man in the picture was round in the waist, had long straight hair, full facial hair, a big bushy beard, and was wearing a tan button-down shirt, baggy tan pants, and a pair of small round-framed reading glasses. There was an arm around his shoulder, revealing that someone had been standing next to him in the full picture. Atlas handed the picture to Lilou. "Do you think this could be my father?" he said.

"Could be … but where is he?" she said. "I've never seen pictures of any city that looked like this." Lilou handed the picture to Nico.

Atlas reached back into the box and grabbed the second item. It was an odd-looking pendant attached to a thin metal chain. The pendant was circular and metallic. It had a golden hue and fit in the palm of Atlas's hand. On the surface of the pendant were three strange markings. And at its center was a small and shiny green glass-like circle, like the lens of a small camera.

"What's this? It looks like a necklace, but it's a bit bulky to wear around your neck, don't you think?" Atlas asked, looking at Lilou for confirmation.

"I would never wear that hideous thing," she responded, cringing.

Atlas handed her the pendant. To his surprise, she passed it to Nico without taking a second look.

"The symbols on this pendant are strange. It looks like some sort of hieroglyph, but I don't recognize the characters," Nico mumbled. He seemed to be the only one interested in it.

The last item Atlas pulled from the box was a small note. On it were two series of numbers, interspersed with dots and dashes. "Nico, can you make any sense of this?" Atlas asked. If anyone could, he thought it would be Nico.

Nico examined it. "They almost look like coordinates, but I don't recognize the format."

"Coordinates?" Atlas asked.

"Coordinates, you know, like on a map. You have coordinates for the x-axis and coordinates for the y-axis, and if you put the two of them together, you can get an exact location on a two-dimensional space," Nico explained.

"Wait, what time is it?" Atlas asked.

"It's seven o'clock. The bus will be here in ten minutes," Nico replied.

"Then we should go now," Atlas declared. Lilou looked confused. "Wait ... Go where?"

"To find Dr. Faraday, remember? The man said he would have the answers. Well, what are we waiting for?" Atlas asked excitedly.

"You're not gonna tell Mom we're missing school?" Lilou said.

"She'll never find out. We'll be back at our normal time, I promise," Atlas assured her.

"Well, we should at least tell her we're riding our bikes today," Lilou said.

"Can you please tell her? I don't want to."

"Me? This is your crazy plan. You tell her," Lilou retorted.

"Okay, how about we Rock, Paper, Scissors for it?" Atlas suggested, knowing it was his only chance of getting out of it.

"Fine, but only because I think I'm better than you at Rock, Paper, Scissors," Lilou replied as she placed her fist in her hand. "Ready?"

"Ready," Atlas replied, holding up his fist.

"Rock ... Paper ... Scissors ... Shoot!" Atlas and Lilou shouted simultaneously.

Lilou smirked at Atlas. "Ha! Paper beats Rock. Go tell Mom we're leaving. And you better make up a good excuse for why we're not taking the bus."

"Fine ... I will," Atlas replied with a sigh. "Now, what are we supposed to do with these?" he said, motioning to the items on the table.

"Mom clearly wanted you to have them. We should take them with us," Nico suggested.

Each of them picked up one item from the table. Atlas placed the photograph in the front pocket of his jeans; Lilou grudgingly threw the large pendant into her bag; and Nico put the note into his backpack. Lilou and Nico headed to the garage. Atlas walked to the foot of the banister.

"Mom!" he called up the stairs.

She appeared at the top of the staircase. "Hey, you. I know it wasn't much, but I hope it helps to have something from your birth mother," she said.

"Oh, right. Yeah, thanks, I really appreciate it," Atlas said, distracted. "Say, I think we're gonna head off now and ride our bikes to school today, if that's all right?" he asked, trying to sound nonchalant.

"Your bikes? Why aren't you taking the bus? Did something happen?" Adora asked.

"Yeah ... something like that. Can we just ride our bikes today?" Atlas repeated.

"Of course, it's not a problem. Say, where are Lilou and Nico? Did you kids eat the pancakes I made?" Adora asked, looking over the banister for them.

"They're waiting outside. I think we're gonna grab something to eat at school."

"All right. When you get home, we will make that appointment with Dr. Faraday. I promise."

Atlas nodded and smiled before heading out the front door. Lilou and Nico were waiting at the side of the house with his bike.

"Are we good?" Lilou asked.

"Yeah, we're good."

The three hopped on their bikes and headed toward the university.

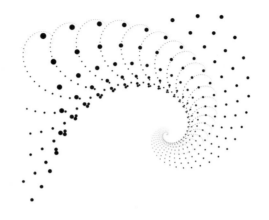

Chapter 3

As the siblings rode across town to Boise State University, Atlas hoped Dr. Faraday would have answers for him. Before he'd received the box from Adora, his only clue that the voice might be his father's was that he'd called Atlas *"my child."* Now that Atlas had the photograph, he felt more confident about Nico's hypothesis.

The kids headed straight for the university's administration building. Seeing three young middle school aged kids in front of her on a school day, the clerk at the reception desk looked confused.

She checked her calendar of events. "Are you kids here for a field trip?"

"No, we're here to see Dr. Faraday," Atlas said.

"Dr. Faraday. Can I ask what for?" the clerk said, raising an eyebrow.

"We need to speak with him about ..." Atlas drew a blank.

"He's my uncle," Lilou said. "He offered to give us a tour of the campus. We're thinking of coming here someday. Maybe even early. My brother here is a bit of a genius. Aren't you, Nico?"

Nico was flipping through the brochures on the desk in front of him and didn't look up.

The clerk looked at the kids again, then at her staff directory. "I don't know if Dr. Faraday is in, but his office is Room 208 in that building over there." She pointed out the window to a tall building across the lawn.

Lilou beamed at her. "Oh, perfect. Thank you so much. Have a great day!"

The three left before the receptionist could ask any more questions. They walked across the lawn and into the tall building.

"Atlas, what will you say to him when we find him?" Lilou asked.

Realizing he hadn't thought that far ahead, Atlas replied, "I guess I'll ask if he knew my father."

"Bold. I like it," Lilou responded, nodding her head in approval.

Standing in front of Room 208, Atlas took a deep breath before knocking.

Knock, Knock.

"My office hours are not for another ten minutes. Go away!" a voice yelled from inside.

The kids looked at each other, wondering what to do next.

Finally, Atlas spoke. "Excuse me, Dr. Faraday. I'm not one of your students. I just have a few questions to ask you."

They heard heavy footsteps, then the door swung open. "Who did you say you were?" The man inside the door stood nearly six one. His dark brown hair was cut short. He wore black, square-framed glasses, a blue button-down shirt and khaki shorts that made him look semi-professional. He also looked agitated.

"Oh ... well, my name is Atlas, and this is Lilou and —" Atlas started to explain.

"I'm sorry. I meant, what are you doing here?"

"I have a few questions for you. I was told that you might have the answers," Atlas said.

"Answers to what? How old are you kids, anyway?" he asked.

"We're twelve," Atlas said sheepishly.

"Twelve? You're almost as tall as me, kid. Now *he* might be twelve," Dr. Faraday said, motioning to Nico, who was standing behind Atlas and Lilou.

Atlas, realizing the conversation wasn't off to a great start, pulled out the picture from his front pocket. He held it out to Dr. Faraday. "Sir, I believe this is my father. Did you know him?"

"Let me see," the professor said, taking the photo. "Where was this picture taken? They must be in front of a green screen. This background is very peculiar." He took a step back, accidentally allowing the kids to enter his office. "I'm sorry, but no. I've never seen this man before."

"Are you sure? Maybe the two of you used to work together?" Atlas asked, desperation in his voice.

"I seriously doubt it, but this photo looks pretty old. What did you say his name was?"

"I'm sorry. I don't know his name ..." Atlas said, looking down at the floor.

Nico, who had been wandering around the office staring at the pictures on the walls, as well as the many books stacked on the shelves and piled on chairs, butted in. "I'm confused. Your door says you're a professor of art history, yet all your books are about quantum and theoretical physics. And this picture looks like some kind of model. Is this string theory?"

Dr. Faraday threw a puzzled look at Nico before returning his attention back to Atlas. "Look, kid, like I said, I don't know your father. Is there some thing else I can help you kids with? I'm very busy," he said, handing the photo back to Atlas.

Lilou stepped forward. "Listen," she said, "this is my brother, Atlas. He's looking for his father, who we believe is the man in that picture. That man appeared out of thin air in our bedroom this morning and told us to find you. So here we are."

"What do you mean, he appeared out of thin air?"

"She means he opened a wormhole and talked to us. Kind of like this one," Nico said. He pointed to a picture of a wormhole in a book he'd taken off a shelf.

The professor looked annoyed. "There is no such thing as a wormhole, kid, and definitely not any that could fit inside a kid's bedroom."

"If there is no such thing as a wormhole, why did you write a book about them?" Nico said, holding up the back cover of the book. Beneath an over size portrait of the professor was printed the name, Dr. Malcolm Faraday, Professor of Theoretical Physics.

"Hey, put that down! Can you please stop touching my things."

"I think you're not telling us everything you know ... Malcolm, is it?" Lilou boldly asked.

"It's still Dr. Faraday to you, kid," he responded.

"Do you even teach art history?" Atlas asked.

"I do now," Faraday replied. He sounded disappointed in himself.

"What do you mean, 'you do now'? Did something happen?" Atlas asked.

Dr. Faraday glanced at the open door. "I don't typically share my life issues with a bunch of strange kids who show up out of the blue." Faraday peaked into the hall, and then shut the door. "But if it means I won't have to answer the door for any of my students today, then why not."

Faraday spun a small globe on the corner of his desk with his fingers as he walked around the desk and sat in a large leather chair. He gestured for the kids to sit on the couch against the wall.

Knock, knock, knock.

"Go away! My office hours are cancelled!" the professor shouted. He opened a desk drawer and pulled out a flask. "Where was I?" he asked as he took a sip from it. "Ah, yes. As I just explained, I didn't always teach art history. Before this, I taught physics at Stanford University for ten years. I was also the head of the Stanford Institute for Theoretical Physics. We were a team of professors who researched high energy and condensed matter based on quantum field and string theory. We were trying to prove the existence of wormholes and their possible application for interdimensional travel.

"We were close to succeeding, but unfortunately, one of our experiments went very wrong. Many people got hurt, and one person even perished — or so they believe. I had my own theories. Anyway ... that doesn't matter. Our funding was pulled; the institute was shut down, and I lost my tenure. After that, I decided to move back to my hometown. Which brings me to where I am today — teaching art history at Boise State. And here's a little secret." Faraday leaned across the table and lowered his voice. "The only Van Gogh painting I know anything about is *Starry Night*."

"*Sunflowers* was always my favorite," Nico put in. His face was still buried in Faraday's book.

The professor looked at Nico, bewildered.

Atlas stood. "Listen, you must be the person we're looking for. I know this sounds crazy, but it's all true. The past few months I've been getting bad migraines, and now they're getting worse. Yesterday, in the middle of science class, I heard a voice in my head. This morning, the same voice woke me up. Then a man appeared in my sister's bedroom and told me I needed to find him before it was too late, and that *you* would have the answers."

Faraday sat back in his chair, taking in everything he'd just heard. "Okay. Let's say for the moment

I believe everything you've told me. I still don't understand what this has to do with me."

"I don't know why he told me to find you, but don't you think it's odd that you study wormholes and quantum physics?" Atlas replied intently.

"I used to, kid. I study art history now, remember?"

Atlas continued, unfazed. "He must have sent me to you because he believes you can help us open one of those wormholes and find him."

"Open a wormhole? Find him? You can't just open a wormhole. Are you hearing yourself?" Faraday leaned forward in his chair.

"Your research. You said you were close," Atlas reminded him.

"Even if we were close, it doesn't matter now. It's all gone; my research, the lab, everything — gone." Faraday stood, looking ready to usher the kids out the door.

"You say here in your book that every point in spacetime has a frequency, and if you could tap into that frequency, you could create a gateway between dimensions," Nico said, holding up a book titled *Vibrations and Frequencies: The Secrets to the Universe,* that he'd been reading during the conversation. He was already about a quarter of the way through.

"Is that true, Dr. Faraday?" Atlas asked.

The professor leaned back in his chair. "It was just a hypothesis. We were never able to test it. The frequencies I talked about are not something you can create with just any instrument — they're quantum frequencies. We believed that the universe was made up of a series of interlacing cosmic strings, which, if vibrated, could open wormholes through spacetime. But we were missing something. We couldn't produce the energy needed to stabilize the wormhole, and our attempt to open one proved fatal.

"So unless you have any other information you haven't shared, I can't help you. I'm sorry. I hope you find the answers you're looking for. I really do," Faraday concluded. He went to the door and opened it.

Atlas took the hint and walked out of the office, followed by his siblings. He turned around to make one last attempt to speak to Faraday, but the door was already closed.

Feeling dejected, they walked back to the administration building.

"Maybe he wasn't the right Dr. Faraday," Lilou said. "Remember, Atlas, you said you found a lot of Dr. Faradays on the internet. Let's go home, reset, and see where we can find the next closest one," she suggested.

"He sure knew an awful lot about theoretical physics and wormholes," Nico reminded them.

"Nico's right. He *was* the right one. But if the voice was my father's, he was wrong. Dr. Faraday didn't have answers. Can we just go home?" Atlas implored them.

The kids pedaled home in silence. Lilou and Nico headed into the house, followed by Atlas. Adora, who was standing in the foyer, stopped him.

"Nico just told me you guys skipped school to go to the university. Is that true?" Adora sounded disappointed.

"We went to see Dr. Faraday, but he couldn't help me," Atlas said, his eyes down as he walked up the stairs.

"Atlas, wait!" Adora cried.

"What?" Atlas stopped. He sounded annoyed.

"You didn't tell me you were going to see him today. I thought you were going to school. We agreed we would call him after school and make an appointment. I told you I didn't mind if you wanted to search for your father. I even said I'd help, and this is how you repay me, by skipping school and lying to me?"

"Why do you care, anyway?" Atlas asked, staring at the floor.

"Why do I care? I care because I'm your mother, that's why," Adora retorted.

"Hardly ..."

Adora placed her hands on her hips. "Excuse me?"

"You're not my real mom, you're just my adopted mom. I've lived with foster parents longer than with you," Atlas said, knowing full well that would hurt Adora the most.

"I'm not your real mom? Atlas, if that's true, it's because you haven't let me be. You have to stop shutting me out. Can't you see I want to help you?"

"You can't help me. Nobody can," Atlas said dejectedly.

"Fine, if that's how you feel, go and find this father of yours. I've already told you, there was nobody else there at the hospital, and nobody came looking for your birth mom. But if you want to chase a ghost, be my guest." Adora walked away. She looked both hurt and angry.

Atlas ran to his room, threw his backpack on the floor, jumped on his bed, and buried his face in his pillow. He was confused and angry, and he didn't know who to be angry at. He was mad that he still didn't have answers about the voice in his head, that he didn't know whether the man he saw was his father, and that Dr. Faraday didn't have the answers he needed. Most of all, he was upset that despite having Lilou and Nico, he still felt alone.

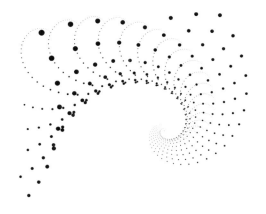

Chapter 4

Atlas woke up feeling upset and ashamed that he'd hurt Adora. He'd attacked her. She didn't deserve that, but he didn't have the courage to apologize. He decided to skip breakfast and sneak out through the garage. He crawled out of bed, put on the clothes he'd worn the day before, grabbed his backpack, and crept down the stairs. As he walked to the garage, he heard Adora, Lilou, and Nico talking in the kitchen. "Okay, Mom. Don't worry. We will," he heard Lilou say.

"And remember, you come straight home. You understand?" Adora insisted.

Before he could reach for the doorknob and escape, Lilou and Nico walked out of the kitchen.

"Where do you think you're going?" Lilou snapped.

"I thought I'd ride my bike today," Atlas replied, avoiding eye contact.

"Ha, not a chance. Mom told us we had to take the bus to school after that little stunt we pulled yesterday," she replied.

Great, could this week get any worse? Atlas thought as he followed Lilou and Nico to the bus stop.

"Also, I heard that fight you got into with Mom. That wasn't cool," Lilou said, crossing her arms.

"Yeah, I know. I'll apologize when we get home today," Atlas said, feeling ashamed and guilty.

When the bus arrived, the kids once again took the seats at the front. Atlas glanced at the back to see if Zach was sitting there. To Atlas's disappointment, he was. Luckily, he didn't seem interested in making another scene, because he ignored them.

When they arrived at school, Lilou headed to their first class without saying goodbye.

"See you at lunch, Atlas?" Nico asked.

"Yeah ... see you at lunch," Atlas replied apathetically.

Atlas made it through his morning classes without any issues. He began to think the day wouldn't be so bad. He went over his encounter with Dr. Faraday. Had he asked the right questions? Dr. Faraday clearly didn't recognize his father from the photo and obviously didn't know how to open a wormhole. *Why would my father send me to find Dr. Faraday if he didn't have any answers?*

Atlas pulled the torn photograph out of his front pocket and took another look at the man he believed to be his father. It was hard to see the man's features, because his facial hair, and shaggy beard covered most of his face. As Atlas continued studying the photo, he saw something he hadn't noticed before. His father was wearing the pendant from the box around his neck. *Wait, the necklace belonged to my father?*

Atlas tried to recall where the pendant was. He remembered that the last time he'd seen it, Lilou had thrown it into her bag. He waited eagerly for the lunch bell and hurried to the cafeteria so he could take another look at it. Lilou and Nico were sitting at the same table where they'd sat on the first day.

"Lilou, do you have the necklace from the box?" Atlas asked straightaway.

"I think so. Let me check my bag. Why, what's up?"

"Look at the picture again. Look at what he's wearing around his neck." Atlas pulled out the photo and showed it to her.

"Okay. So, he's wearing the necklace. What's the big deal?" Lilou said dismissively.

"Come on, it can't be a coincidence. My father must have wanted me to find it," Atlas said, tapping his foot with impatience.

Lilou reached into her bag and pulled out the pendant. "Here, take it. I was tired of lugging that thing around, anyway."

Atlas was taking a closer look at the pendant when Nico said excitedly, "Look, it says right here that Dr. Faraday was working on building a device that could create the quantum frequencies needed to open a wormhole. His problem was finding a stable power source. There's even a sketch of what he thought the device might look like."

"Wait-what are you reading?" Atlas asked.

"Dr. Faraday's book."

"You took his book from his office?" Atlas wondered how he could have missed that.

"Yeah. I'll return it when I'm done. I promise. It's fascinating stuff."

"Let me see it." Atlas reached across the table and grabbed the book from Nico.

Atlas read the section Nico had mentioned and looked at the sketch. He looked back and forth between the sketch and the pendant. "Look. This device in the sketch looks a lot like this necklace."

The kids were leaning over the page to get a better look when they heard someone shout, "Who said that!" from a nearby table. They turned to see where the voice had come from. Zach was standing on top of one of the cafeteria tables, pretending to look around in confusion. Everyone in the room started laughing. Soon, all eyes were on the siblings.

"What are they laughing at?" Nico asked.

"Oh, Nico," Lilou said. "You've got the book smarts down, but you've got to work on your street smarts. They're laughing at Atlas."

She started to stand to reprimand Zack, but Atlas shot up and beat her to it. "Is there a problem?"

"Yeah, I have a problem. Why did you and your little band of orphans come to my school?" Zach said, throwing them a disgusted look as he jumped off the table.

"Okay, that's it," Lilou whispered. She stood and faced the bully. "I'm surprised they haven't kicked you out of this school already. How many times have you been expelled, twice is it?" she asked.

Ignoring Lilou's comment, Zach started to goad the three. "What a surprise. Your sister is speaking up for you again. Say, I couldn't help but notice you don't look like your brother and sister. Did they adopt you, or did you adopt them? I'm not really sure how this all works," Zach snickered.

An explosion of laughter followed from all the seventh graders in the cafeteria.

All the taunts Atlas had ever endured at different schools came back to him. He turned red in the face. Frustrated that he couldn't come up with a quick response, Atlas picked up his tray of food and threw it at Zach.

Time seemed to slow as Atlas, Lilou, Nico, and the rest of the students watched the tray of fried chicken, mashed potatoes, and chocolate milk soar through the air. The drumstick catapulted away from the tray, smacking Zach square in the eye, and the mashed potatoes and milk splattered across his face and chest like shrapnel. Zach stood still as the sea of students stared. They covered their mouths with their hands in shock, as if they'd witnessed a murder. Before Zach had a chance to wipe the milk from his face, the siblings sprinted out of the cafeteria. Behind them, they heard Zach yell, "Get back here, Stretch!"

They streaked down the hall, looking for a place to hide. "Where are we going?" Nico shouted from behind.

"Quick, in here," Lilou said, directing them through an open doorway.

They found themselves in the school's small theater. "Back there! Behind the curtains," Atlas ordered. They ran behind the curtains and hid in a small back stage corner. They heard footsteps outside the door, but they were unsure if they belonged to Zach or a school staff member.

"What are we supposed to do now?" Atlas asked nervously.

"We wait here until the coast is clear, and then we head home," Lilou replied.

As Atlas looked out from behind the curtain to see who was there, he felt the pendant in his pocket. *I must have grabbed it as we left the room,* he thought. He pulled it out and said, "The necklace. It looks just like the sketch from Dr. Faraday's book, doesn't it?"

Lilou looked puzzled. "It did look a lot like that sketch, but what does that mean?"

Atlas inspected the pendant, feeling around its edges. "Look, right here. I think I found something." He pointed to a small, raised marking on the back of the necklace.

"Well, push it," Lilou said impatiently.

Atlas did. Suddenly, the necklace came to life, emitting a neon green light from its center. Surprised, Atlas let go of it, and it fell to the floor. The green light slowly created an image in the air that filled the entire stage. It appeared to be a hologram, displaying countless green lights connected like a web of interconnected strings.

The siblings froze, staring at each other and the hologram.

"What are we looking at?" Lilou asked, perplexed.

Atlas walked around the image slowly, observing every inch of it. "Dr. Faraday said the universe was made up of cosmic strings. I think this could be a map of the universe."

"Well, not exactly," Nico corrected him. "Look, each of these clusters of strings is a universe. We're not looking at one universe. We're looking at a multiverse," he said, his eyes wide with excitement.

A multiverse? Atlas thought.

"Look, there's a keyboard." Lilou pointed at what looked like a small holographic keyboard radiating from the side of the device.

Atlas turned to Nico. "Do you remember what Dr. Faraday said about vibrations and frequencies?" he said, hoping he was onto something.

"Yes. He said if you could pinpoint a frequency and vibrate the cosmic strings, it would open a wormhole. But he said it was a hypothesis."

Just then, they heard someone enter the theater. "Hey, Orphan Boy! I know you and your little siblings are in here."

Lilou placed her hand on the curtain, ready to swing it open and confront Zach, but Atlas stopped her. "No, wait," he whispered.

He heard Zach walk down the aisle toward the stage. "You'll pay for what you did!" Zach taunted them.

Atlas looked at Nico and hissed, "The note. Where is it?"

Nico reached into his backpack and pulled it out.

Please let this work, Atlas thought. He bent and typed in the first set of numbers into the keyboard.

Suddenly, two points on the hologram lit up, and a pathway formed between them. Then the hologram transformed into a bright light that tore open the space on the stage in front of them — revealing a portal. Atlas placed the note in his back pocket, put the device around his neck, and threw open the curtains, fully exposing the portal.

Zach stood in the aisle. He looked hypnotized by the portal's iridescent colors. Coming out of his trance, Zach made eye contact with Atlas, then sprinted toward the stage.

With no hesitation, Atlas grabbed Lilou and Nico's hands and pulled them into the light.

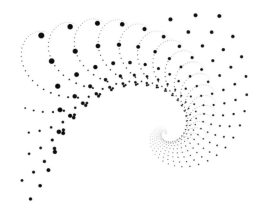

Chapter 5

Materializing on the other side of the wormhole, the siblings found themselves in a large cornfield near a small farmhouse. Atlas, who had fallen face down, pushed off the ground with his hands and stood. "Where are we?" he asked.

Lilou, who had also fallen, stood and gained her footing. "If I said we weren't in Kansas anymore, would that be too cliche?" she asked rhetorically.

Atlas looked at Nico, who was on his knees, staring intently at something off in the distance. Atlas followed Nico's line of sight over the three-foot-high corn stalks, past the farmhouse, and along the horizon, where he spotted a city with massive skyscrapers. Even the smallest building in the skyline appeared more substantial than the tallest building they had seen back in San Diego.

The buildings came in a variety of odd shapes and colors. Many of the buildings were broad and dome-shaped, while others were tall and slender. The taller, more prominent buildings were vibrantly lit by assorted neon-colored lights that appeared to accentuate the buildings' outlines.

Lilou found herself laughing. "Do either of you know what city that is?" she said, knowing none of them had ever seen anything like it before.

"It looks like the city from the photograph," Atlas said, hoping that meant they were close to finding his father.

"Hmm ... that's strange," Nico said, bending to touch a young green shoot at his feet. "This looks like a typical corn stalk. That means we must be standing in a regular cornfield."

As they began to take in more of their surroundings, they decided that things didn't look so strange after all. There was blue sky, white clouds, and the familiar sun starting to set on the horizon behind them. The more they looked, the more they recognized.

"Wait, are we still on Earth?" Atlas asked. "Everything, including this stalk, feels familiar, but by the looks of that city, I'd have to say no," Nico replied, rubbing the silky stalk between his fingers.

Atlas, who had re-focused his attention on the skyline, noticed something moving along the horizon. "Umm, guys, what are those?" he said, pointing. "They look like they're coming this way," he added with concern.

Lilou quickly saw what Atlas was staring at. "Yeah, and fast," she said.

In the distance, four hovering vehicles appeared to be moving toward them at great speed. The vehicles were matte black, long and rectangular, with no wings or noticeable propulsion system. They looked large enough to transport dozens of passengers. Within seconds, the vehicles were on top of them, circling the siblings and creating a perimeter as they began shining spotlights on their position. Atlas tried to read the insignia printed in large white letters on the vehicles' hulls, but the lights were too bright for him to make them out. Suddenly, a hatch on the bottom of one of the vehicles opened, revealing a man in a white suit, standing on the ramp of the craft. The man pointed at them. His voice blared from all four vehicles at once: "You three! Stay where you are. Don't move!"

"Who are these guys?" Atlas said, wondering if they'd just made a big mistake.

"I have no idea, but they don't look very friendly," Lilou replied.

"If I had to guess, I'd say they're the local police," Nico added, unfazed.

Atlas and Lilou looked at him in bewilderment, wondering how he was able to stay calm and collected.

All the vehicles hovered just above the cornfield, then touched down. The remaining hatches opened and heavily armed men in uniform came rushing out. The men looked and moved like soldiers the kids had seen in movies, and were equipped with heavy, black-plated body armor and bulky black rifles.

"Get on your knees and put your hands above your head! Do as I say, now!" one screamed.

As Lilou, Nico, and Atlas followed the soldier's directions, one of Atlas's hands inadvertently brushed against the device around his neck. He glanced down and gave it a slight squeeze.

"You there, get your hand away from the transponder, and put your hands above your head!" another soldier shouted.

So, it's called a transponder, Atlas thought. He took his hand off it and put his arms up.

One of the soldiers snatched the device off Atlas's neck and trotted back toward the man in the white suit. He was standing ten yards away in the cornfield, keeping his distance, but close enough for the kids to hear him speak. "I have the transponder you asked for, sir," the soldier said.

"Good, give it to me." The man took a careful look at the transponder and then placed the device around his neck. "What are you waiting for?" he snapped. "Get bindings on them, search them, and throw them on one of the transports."

Within moments, the soldiers began stripping the kids of their backpacks and belongings.

"Hey! Get your hands off me!" Lilou shouted, as a soldier tugged off her backpack.

"Excuse me sir, can you please take care of my book ..." Nico started to say, as a second soldier walked off with his things.

The soldiers bound the kids' hands behind their backs and shoved them into a transport filled with soldiers. It effortlessly lifted off the ground and sped toward the city.

Inside, the siblings sat frozen in silence, observing their surroundings.

Who are they, and where are they taking us? Atlas thought. He spotted a large patch sewn across the chest of the soldier across from him. "P.O.R.T.A.L.? What does that stand for?" he asked.

The soldier, surprised by this display of courage, smirked at Atlas. "You don't know? We are the Protectors Of Realm Transportation And Logistics," he scoffed.

"Wow, you guys really made that acronym work," Lilou interjected. "I'm impressed," she added honestly.

"Can I ask where we are we going?" Atlas said.

"To the Central Hub. Now keep your mouths shut, both of you!" the soldier commanded them.

"I'm sorry. I have one last question, which my brother should have started with," Lilou said, with a nervous laugh. *"Where* are we?"

The soldier, appearing annoyed, simply gestured toward the window behind them.

The siblings turned and looked out the window just in time to see a huge floating neon sign that displayed the words WELCOME TO BOISE. The S in Boise flickered on and off.

Atlas and Nico stared at it in disbelief. Lilou shook her head, looking stunned, and whispered, "You've got to be kidding me."

The transport rose in elevation as it got closer to the city and floated over the top of the skyscrapers. As they went deeper into the endless field of skyscrapers, they saw numerous flying crafts weaving around each other and the buildings. More large neon signs were floating in the air. They displayed an array of information and were all written in plain English.

Soon, the transport approached a massive rectangular building at the city's center. The word P.O.R.T.A.L. was illuminated in bold white letters down its side. When they arrived at the top, a huge hangar door opened, and the transport landed gently inside.

The siblings were shocked to see an entire fleet of transport ships and what appeared to be smaller, two-person fighter crafts in the hangar. A small squadron of soldiers escorted them off the ship and into the building's interior, where they were led through a long maze of curved, cylindrical white corridors lit by two rows of paneled lights on either wall. They passed more soldiers who appeared to be on patrol but were uninterested in their presence.

When they came to a halt, they were shepherded into a small white room. It contained one small rectangular table surrounded by five metallic chairs. The soldiers forced them into the seats and exited the room.

When the last soldier closed the door behind him, Atlas turned to his siblings with a frown. "Who are these guys, and what do you think they want with us?"

"I have no idea, but they don't seem happy with us being here," Lilou replied uneasily.

"And why do they have us in this small room?" Atlas added.

"If I had to guess, this is their interrogation room," Nico replied, looking around for a two-way mirror.

Just then, the man in the white suit walked in and started pacing around the room. He was skinnier than he'd appeared from a distance. His blond hair was slicked back and a pair of small circular shades that hid his eyes rested on his pointy nose. After what felt like an eternity, he stopped in front of the table, took a seat, and removed his shades, revealing bright green eyes.

"Here at P.O.R.T.AL, we have a very special job," he said softly. "You see, it's our patriotic duty to monitor and track all interdimensional travel. I have been personally charged with the privilege of protecting this realm from all outside threats. Therefore, when I detected your unauthorized wormhole outside of our beautiful city of Boise, I was quite displeased. Now, for the record, who are you? Where are you from? And what are you doing here?" The man spoke in an oddly calm manner.

Atlas glanced at his siblings and realized he would have to speak for them. "My name is Atlas, and this is my sister, Lilou, and my brother, Nico. We're from Boise, Idaho, and we're looking for my father," Atlas answered with a slight tremor in his voice.

The man stood and placed his hand on his chin. "You're from Boise, huh? What are the chances ..." He trailed off with a distant look in his eyes.

He soon returned from his thoughts and resumed pacing. "None of that information does me any good. If you haven't figured it out yet, this is Earth, but not your Earth. There are billions of earths, and I need to know which of them you three are from. Depending on which one you're from, you could be given a slap on the wrist for unauthorized travel or thrown in prison for the rest of your lives.

"You see, interdimensional travel is a very tricky thing, and can cause major problems when one isn't expecting ... visitors. That's why the Council prohibits interdimensional travel to and from all realms that are not part of the System.

"The transponder you were wearing is from our realm, not yours. So, where did you get it?" he asked Atlas, clearly annoyed.

Suddenly, the door opened. A soldier entered the room and whispered loudly into the man's ear, "Sir, you might want to see this."

The man in the suit appeared irritated. He looked at the kids and put up one finger to indicate he would need a moment. The soldier handed him a small item. The siblings tried to catch a glimpse of it, but the man's back blocked their view. He took the item, looked at it closely, and then looked back at the kids suspiciously. He whispered something to the soldier, who left the room. After taking another look at the item, the man calmly returned to the table. His demeanor changed as he slammed a photograph on the table. *"How do you know The Fugitive!"* he screamed. Large veins protruded from the sides of his neck.

Atlas looked at the torn photograph of his father. He must be the fugitive the man meant. *It's never good when they refer to someone as The Fugitive,* Atlas thought.

"That's my father," Atlas said with feigned confidence. "He's the man we're looking for, and he's the reason we're here." Atlas immediately wondered if this might have been a good time to lie.

The man stood and casually adjusted his collar, as if disappointed in himself for losing his temper. His veins slowly receded. "Well, that makes two of us, doesn't it?" he replied, picking the photo up and placing it in his front pocket. He began to pace again. "Your father, you say? I wasn't aware that Elio had a child. How old did you say you were?"

Atlas glared at him. "We're twelve. Now, what do you want with him?"

"Interesting, interesting indeed. You three really don't know anything about him, do you? That man is the most wanted man in the Multiverse. As I explained before, interdimensional travel is strictly prohibited to realms outside the System. That man defied the Council's rule and made contact with unknown realms. To make matters worse, your father was selling our technology and profiting from it. When we find him, he will spend an eternity in Purgatory. Do you understand me?" the man shouted.

"That can't be true. Take it back!" Atlas stood and shouted back, not understanding why he felt so infuriated.

The man in the white suit returned to his calm self. "And how would you know, exactly? Do you even know your father? I'm sorry to be the one to break it to you, but your father is a criminal." The man grabbed the photo off the table and calmly walked back toward the door.

Lilou stood and yelled, "What's going to happen to us?"

The man turned back around. "Oh, you three aren't going anywhere. Aside from spending time in prison for breaking interdimensional laws, you're going to help me find your father," he said with a grin, before slamming the door shut behind him.

Moments later, three soldiers entered and handed each of them a tan jumpsuit to change into. The soldiers then hurried them to the prisoners' quarters, within what looked like an endless corridor of cells.

As they walked down a long hall, they passed more corridors spaced out every fifty feet or so, leading to more rows of cells. Each cell they passed had three solid walls and a thick plexiglass door through which they could see the prisoners within.

"There must be hundreds of people here. Do you think they're all here for the same reason as us?" Atlas asked Lilou and Nico.

"Doubtful, but judging by the number of people, I imagine it doesn't take much to end up here," Nico replied.

"What are they doing?" Lilou asked, seeing that many of the prisoners had approached their plexiglass doors and placed their right hand on the glass with their fingers spread wide.

"It looks like they're trying to communicate with us," Nico surmised.

Finally, the soldier motioned for them to stop. "This one here is for the tall one. You two are on the other side," he declared. The soldier pushed a button on his handheld device, and one of the plexiglass windows slid open. Before he could say goodbye, Atlas was shoved into the cell.

Only then did Atlas realize he and his siblings would be separated. This left him with an overwhelming sense of dread.

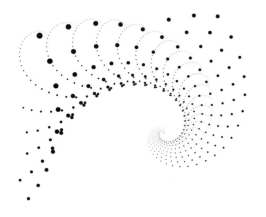

Chapter 6

A tlas, my child, wake up!

    Atlas was again awoken by a voice inside his head. He sat slowly. He'd forgotten he was inside a P.O.R.T.A.L. prison cell. It took a moment for the memories of the last few days to return, but when they did, he was overwhelmed with emotion. Without time to reflect, Atlas stood and looked around to make sure no one else could be speaking to him. He saw nothing but three white walls and a solid plexiglass window.

Atlas, my child, can you hear me?

Realizing that it was indeed his father's voice inside his head, he tried something different. "Father, is that you? Can you hear me?" Atlas asked, using his internal voice.

Yes, my child, I can hear you.

"But how is this happening? How am I able to speak to you inside my head?"

It's a little invention I developed in order to find you. I call it a voice transponder, and it allows me to communicate with you directly. Just as you have probably learned by now that every wormhole in the Multiverse has its own frequency, I have learned that every living thing does as well. And if you can tune into that life-frequency, you can use it to communicate. Think of it as opening a mini-wormhole in your mind.

You see, Atlas, I've spent the last ten years trying to pinpoint your exact frequency. It wasn't easy, but I hypothesized that every living organism's frequency must be similar to that of their parents'. I experimented with different combinations of my own. Even so, it took me ten years to establish a connection with you, but I have finally done it, and for that, I am grateful.

"Ten years? You've been looking for me all this time?" Atlas remembered how lonely he had felt all those years in foster homes.

Why, of course, my son. I have been conducting endless experiments fine-tuning my invention so I might locate you.

"Experiments? Do you think your experiments could have caused something like a migraine?"

Migraine? Yes. I suspect it could have. Perhaps migraines were a side effect of my many attempts at pinpointing your frequency.

"Well, I'm glad you did."

Atlas, how did you end up here? Did Dr. Faraday complete his research? Did he help you open a wormhole?

"No. He didn't help us with anything. We used your transponder and the note with the coordinates on it. They were given to me by my adoptive mother."

I gave that transponder to your mother as a wedding gift. I left it behind by mistake. It was programmed to only respond to your mother's touch. I suspect that because your life-frequency is similar to hers, it allowed you to activate the device. When you used it to open a wormhole, it sent me an alert, and I was able to track your frequency to this realm. As for the note, I don't remember leaving any note. And why would it contain the coordinates to this realm . . .?

"Wait — where are you right now?" Atlas said. He wondered if that meant he was close by.

I'm here looking for you. My voice transponder only works if the subject and I are in the same realm. I have traveled here to establish a connection with you.

"But that would mean, back at my school, in my room, you were there?" Atlas asked, surprised.

Yes, I was there, but I struggled to keep the connection open long enough to track your exact location. I have also been using my invention to develop a new transponder that will be more precise. Right now, transponders only allow one to use existing wormholes to travel between realms using pre-programmed coordinates. To travel to a specific location within any realm, such as a prison cell, you would need a more precise frequency to create a new pathway, but I believe my voice transponder might hold the key.

"What about the portal in our bedroom?" Atlas asked.

Yes, in that instance I was finally able to keep the connection in your mind open long enough to track your location, but unfortunately, the wormhole was unstable, and I couldn't pass through. But I believe my new transponder will soon be ready. When it is, I will be able to use it to travel directly to you.

"That's great! You can use it to rescue me and my siblings from this prison. We were captured by some organization that calls themselves P.O.R.T.A.L.," Atlas responded, feeling hopeful.

Siblings? Atlas, who is there with you?

"Lilou and Nico, my sister and brother. We were all adopted by the same mom," Atlas replied, only now realizing his father couldn't know about his siblings.

This is grave news. You should have never brought them with you. It is too dangerous here. I'm also afraid it won't be easy to get inside P.O.R.T.A.L.'s Central Hub. It has a state-of-the art jamming system. No existing wormhole will open anywhere within their city limits.

Atlas's father paused, then said, *If I could get closer to that building, I might be able to use my new transponder to bypass their jammers. But I need more time. I need to find a way to stabilize the wormhole.*

"Father, who are these people and what do they want with us?" Atlas asked.

It's not you they want, it's me. P.O.R.T.A.L. works for the Council, an evil entity that wants to rule the Multiverse. They control and regulate all interdimensional travel, which gives them the upper hand. However, they don't yet have full control.

You see, there are billions of universes, most of which have not yet been discovered. I have been trying to chart and share my knowledge with those realms. That way, when the time is right, we will have a fighting chance. Wait — do you hear that? They must have tracked me. My position has been compromised. I must go. Stay vigilant, my son. I will be back. Goodbye for now!

"Wait, father, please don't go!" Atlas yelled, forgetting to use his internal voice.

Without warning, the connection was lost, and Atlas was again alone in his cell. He spent the next few hours replaying the conversation in his head and thinking about his siblings and his father. He felt a deep sense of remorse for bringing Lilou and Nico with him, especially after his father explained the danger they were in. Just two days earlier, he'd known nothing about interdimensional travel or the Multiverse, and now he found himself in a strange new world with even more questions.

His father had said P.O.R.T.A.L. was working for the Council, but who were they? And why did they want to rule the Multiverse? Atlas also wondered what his father meant by "a fighting chance." Was his father a rogue criminal, or was he helping people resist the Council's rule? All these questions weighed on Atlas's mind. He wondered if he would find the answers he was looking for.

His father's words had, however, left him with one small glimmer of hope. Perhaps the new transponder might help Atlas and his siblings escape prison. But when? Atlas hoped he'd soon have a chance to speak with Lilou and Nico about this encounter and all that he'd learned, but he didn't know when or, more importantly, *if,* he would be given a chance.

Atlas spent the next few days pacing back and forth, lying on his cot, and resting with his back against the plexiglass, wondering how soon his father would contact him again. His only stimulation came from the daily meals delivered through a small compartment built into the back wall of the cell. Finally, after what felt like an entire week had passed, the plexiglass window slid open.

For a fleeting moment, Atlas wondered if it was his father's doing and whether he had come to rescue him — until he saw the prisoner across from him stand and casually exit his cell. When Atlas approached the door, he saw a line of prisoners, all headed in the same direction. As he watched the prisoners pass by, he realized for the first time that they ranged from young children to the elderly. Hesitantly, he stepped out of his cell and followed the line.

He looked around frantically for Lilou and Nico, but he didn't see them anywhere. As he tried to push his way through the crowd to find them, Atlas accidentally bumped into a girl walking in front of him. She looked to be around his age, but quite a bit shorter, with almond-colored skin and short, black, kinky hair.

The girl, reacting to the hard bump from behind, looked over her shoulder and glared at Atlas. "Excuse you, can I help you with something?"

"I'm sorry. Do you know where we are going?"

"To the gymnasium. It's recreation day, duh."

"Sorry, I'm just new here, is all," Atlas said apologetically.

"I was just messing with you. You'll get the routine down soon enough. It's pretty simple. Once a week, they put us in this big gymnasium to let us exercise or whatever, but most people sit and talk. So thoughtful of them, right?" she said sarcastically.

Intrigued, Atlas wondered how someone could find humor in a place like this. "Will everybody be there?" he asked.

"Why? Are you hoping to meet your girlfriend there or something?" the girl asked, flashing him a smile.

"No," Atlas said, blushing. "I'm looking for my siblings. I haven't seen them in days."

"Oh, are you guys refugees from Earth C19?" she asked sympathetically.

"Earth C19? No, we're not from Earth C19. I don't think ..." Atlas realized he wasn't sure which Earth he was from.

"It's a shame what happened there … but yeah, if they brought you in together, I don't see why they wouldn't be," the girl said optimistically.

The girl's tone calmed Atlas's nerves, and he began to feel more confident that once they got to this gymnasium, he could find his siblings. The corridor eventually ended, and the prisoners turned the corner and piled up behind a large steel door. Slowly, the door creak opened. When it reached the ceiling, it made a loud *bang*. The prisoners pushed their way inside.

Atlas wasn't sure what to expect. The girl had called it a gymnasium, but what he saw was a large, white-domed room with tables spread out every few feet. He thought he saw a faded outline of a track around the perimeter for anyone who wanted to walk or run. Other than that, it looked like a giant mess hall.

Great, I'm back in a school cafeteria. As he had at school, Atlas scanned the room for his siblings.

"Do you see them?" the girl asked him.

Atlas, who'd almost forgotten she was still standing next to him, said, "No, I don't. Wait — I think I see them over there." He pointed across the expansive room to the opposite side. Lilou and Nico were walking in through a different door. Atlas waved and started in their direction when the girl grabbed his shoulder.

"It was nice talking to you," she said.

"Oh right. I'm sorry. I'm just really excited to see them. My name's Atlas. It was nice talking to you, too."

"I'm Mia. Nice meeting you, Atlas. I'll see you around," she said with a smile.

Atlas turned and ran across the great hall to greet his siblings, who didn't see him approach. When Atlas was in earshot, he yelled, "Lilou, Nico, over here!" They turned in time to get a surprise hug from him.

"Atlas! Thank God you're okay." Lilou said. "When they separated us, I thought they took you somewhere … else."

"No. I've been in that same cell all week. Where are your cells?" he asked, wondering why they'd come out of a different door.

"Our cells are behind there," Lilou said, pointing. "They're right across from each other. We can even communicate through the small air holes in the plexiglass window," she added.

"Have you been alone this whole time?" Nico asked with concern.

"Yes, but not entirely … I kind of spoke to my father the other day," Atlas said sheepishly, not sure how they'd react to the news.

"What do you mean, you spoke to your father? He's here?" Lilou said, her eyebrows raised in surprise.

"No, he's not. Okay — you know how I can hear his voice in my head? It turns out, it's a bit more than that. It's more like a two-way radio," Atlas said, afraid they wouldn't believe him.

"Two-way radio? You can talk to him in your mind whenever you want? That's amazing!" Nico exclaimed.

"Well, no, not exactly," Atlas said. "He wants to rescue us, and he's working on another transponder, one that will let him travel anywhere. He said he just needs to figure out how to stabilize the wormhole," Atlas explained, unsure whether he understood it all himself.

"That's great! When did he say he will free us so we can go home?" Lilou asked.

"Well, that's the thing ... He didn't say. P.O.R.T.A.L. tracked him down, and we suddenly lost our connection. I haven't heard from him in a week," Atlas said glumly, staring at the floor.

"Hey, have you guys noticed there are no guards here?" Nico said, looking around the gymnasium.

"No, I hadn't. Why wouldn't there be guards?" Atlas asked. "That's really odd."

"I think it's because guards make sure that prisoners don't escape. If there are no guards, there must be no means of escape," Nico replied.

No means of escape. Atlas scanned their surroundings. It didn't seem like a typical prison. The prisoners appeared relaxed, almost jaded. *Whoever they are, they don't seem like violent types,* Atlas thought. "Have you guys seen anything that looks like an exit?" Atlas said, looking at Nico.

"From what I can tell, there's only one main exit — the door we first walked in," his brother replied. "There seem to be four different blocks, all connected through this big hall, one on each side. You're in the section closest to the exit, and we're on the far side. The only other time I saw a guard was a few days ago when he brought in a new prisoner, but once he put the prisoner in a cell, he left right away."

"I wonder what would happen if we didn't go back to our cells?" Lilou put in.

Nico thought about this. "Hmm. I imagine everyone will, which means we probably don't want to know the answer to that question — though I seriously doubt a guard would come in here," he said.

Lilou grabbed Atlas's arm. "Atlas, you need to talk to your father again. He has to get us out of here. We have to get back home."

"Home? I'm not going home. If my father frees us, I'm going with him. I still have so many questions for him."

"Atlas, what are you talking about?" Lilou said. "Look where we are. We're in prison. These P.O.R.T.A.L. people are dangerous. They found us within five minutes of us coming here. If we don't leave this place, we'll end up right back here."

Atlas looked upset. "Don't you remember how we ended up here in the first place?" he reminded her. "We were about to be pummeled by the school bully."

"The school bully? Are you listening to yourself? That's not how we ended up here. You pulled Nico and me into that ... that ...wormhole. I didn't have a choice, and neither did Nico. If we ever get out of here, we need to get back home to our family," Lilou replied crossly.

"Family? Why do you think I'm here? Who do you think I'm looking for? I'm looking for my family," Atlas reminded her.

"Looking for your family? We are your family," Lilou said, before pausing to take a steadying breath. She continued, "You know, there's something we've never told you before. Nico and I were adopted from the same family. We're fraternal twins, brother and sister by blood. Adora never wanted us to tell you. She thought it would make you jealous or worried that we would treat you differently. The fact that you never realized it shows how much Adora loves you.

"You, Nico, and Adora are my family, and we are your family, too. I don't understand why you still want to look for this ... this person, when so far, all he's done is put you and us in danger. If you really need to find your father, fine. But I won't stick around to watch you get hurt. Come on, Nico, let's go." Lilou grabbed Nico's arm and they started to walk away.

Nico stopped and turned back to Atlas. "When the time comes, I will help you escape with your father, if that's what you want. But afterward, I'll be going back home with Lilou. I'm sorry."

"Guys … wait! Please!" Atlas called out with a pained look. For a moment, he held his breath, hoping they would turn back around and understand why this meant so much to him. But as he watched them disappear into the crowd, he felt his heart sink into his stomach.

Fine, I'll find him on my own. We're probably never getting out of here anyway, he thought. He found an empty table and sat at it. After what felt like minutes, the steel doors reopened, and the prisoners started making their way back to their cells. As Atlas entered the hallway, he ran into Mia, who seemed to be waiting for him.

"Is everything okay? Did you get a chance to talk to your brother and sister?" she said, sounding genuinely interested.

"Yeah. I found them," Atlas replied, avoiding eye contact, hoping to show that he wanted to be left alone. He sped up, entered his cell, heard the door slide shut behind him, and slid down into a heap with his back against the plexiglass window.

He couldn't understand why Lilou wasn't more supportive, because she was the one who always stood up for him at school. As he racked his brain for answers, he thought back to the argument they'd had in her bedroom.

He'd always felt somewhat jealous that Lilou knew her birth parents. But he now understood that her parents were addicts, and that Adora was the most dependable parent she had ever had. He wasn't surprised to learn that Lilou and Nico were fraternal twins. He'd always kind of known this in his heart. Lilou was right, though — neither Adora nor the twins ever treated him differently for it. He realized that Lilou only wanted to protect him from getting hurt, just as she always had.

Atlas's thoughts turned to what Nico had figured out about there being no means of escape. Although it was Nico who had concluded this, Atlas knew that if there was one person who could find a way out of this place, it was Nico.

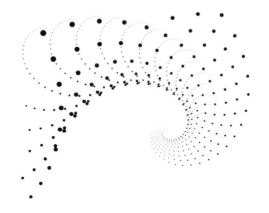

Chapter 7

Atlas sat in his cell, eating his cold and tasteless meal. He was still thinking about his fight with his siblings and debating what he would say the next time he saw them, when he heard his father's voice.

Atlas, can you hear me?

Although surprised to hear from his father, at least now he knew how to respond.

"Yes, I can hear you."

How are you doing, my son? How are they treating you?

The moment his father asked those questions, Atlas sensed that there was no imminent plan to free him. "Your new transponder isn't ready, is it?" he said, unable to hide the disappointment in his voice.

I am afraid it's going to take a little more time. These things can be very complicated. I've been visiting your realm frequently to test how fast P.O.R.TA.L. can track me. After dozens of attempts, I've calculated that they take an average of eight minutes to locate my portal. Their systems are getting more advanced by the day. It once took them hours to track me. I don't know how much longer I can evade them. I fear I will soon find myself caught in a trap.

"Wait — you've been coming here, and you didn't contact me? I've been sitting in this stupid cell for almost two weeks with nobody to talk to."

Atlas, it's not that simple. I couldn't let our communication impact the data. I need to know precisely how much time I will have once my new transponder is finished.

"Why didn't you warn me about P.O.R.T.A.L. I came here looking for you based on your clues."

You're right. I hoped I would be able to find you before they did. It was an acceptable risk.

"Acceptable risk! Is that what this is to you?"

Atlas, it's not like that. Please understand.

"There's nothing to understand. Just go. Leave me alone. P.O.R.T.A.L. has probably already tracked you by now anyway. Goodbye!"

I will be back in three weeks, Atlas. You hear me, three weeks. I promise! His father's voice faded away.

Atlas took the silence that followed to mean that his father had ended their connection. Although he was the one to say "goodbye," Atlas had hoped his father would have wanted to say more, but it seemed he didn't feel the need to apologize. Atlas then remembered that he hadn't apologized to Adora for their fight before they left. He thought about how Adora might be feeling back home, likely desperately looking for her missing children. Atlas hoped she wouldn't think he ran away because of their fight, but he knew that was probably the best scenario she could cling to.

As days passed, Atlas almost lost track of time, but he knew gymnasium day would come soon and with it, the opportunity to smooth things over with Lilou and Nico. He thought a lot about what he would say to them but wondered if they'd be willing to give him a chance. He was also beginning to question whether he wanted to go with his father if he did escape, even though the idea of escaping seemed less likely by the day. Finally, without warning, his cell door opened.

He realized it had been a full week since gymnasium day. Atlas entered the corridor. Hurrying toward the steel door, he spotted Mia up ahead. She appeared to be waiting for him.

She waved him down. "Atlas, over here. Do you want to walk together?"

"Yeah. That would be nice," Atlas replied, happy to have someone to talk to again.

"How are you holding up?"

"I'm all right, I guess," he said, not wanting to talk about his feelings. "How about you?"

She shrugged her shoulders. "Oh, you know, after a year here, you kinda get used to it."

Atlas stopped in his tracks. "Wait, you've been here a year?"

"Yeah, something like that. I've lost track of time," Mia said, gesturing for him to keep walking.

"I-I don't know what to say. I'm really sorry to hear that," Atlas said as they passed through the door.

"Do you see your brother and sister?"

Atlas scanned the room. They were at a table near where he had last spoken to them.

He pointed. "Yeah, I see them over there."

"Well, aren't you gonna go over and talk to them?"

"Oh yeah. Right." He walked nervously toward their table, with Mia by his side.

Lilou looked up and started right in. "So, do you have anything you might want to say to us?"

Atlas turned to Mia. "Hey, do you think you could give us a minute?"

"Yeah, sure, of course," she replied, quietly backing away.

Atlas faced Lilou. "Look, I'm really sorry about last week. I shouldn't have gotten mad at you for wanting to go home. You're right. This place is dangerous, and I should have never dragged either of you into this. I'm not even sure if I know what I want anymore. But I do know we can't wait around for my father to get us out of here."

"You spoke to him again, didn't you?" Nico asked, obviously having heard the change in Atlas's attitude.

"Yeah, a few days ago. He hasn't made any progress on his new transponder. I'm afraid we're on our own."

Lilou, who looked like she was starting to feel bad, jumped back in. "Atlas, I'm sorry too. I promise I'm not trying to keep you from finding your father. I just want to make sure everyone gets home safely and that you see that we're your family too."

"I know," Atlas replied sincerely. "And I care about you both."

"So, who is your little friend?" Lilou asked, motioning to the table behind Atlas.

"Oh, that's Mia," he replied."We talked last week. She's cool. She seems to know a lot about this place. She's been here a long time."

"Well, what are you waiting for? Aren't you going to invite her over?" Lilou said, noticing that Mia was looking at them eagerly.

"Would that be all right with you guys?"

They nodded, and Atlas beckoned to Mia. She sprang up and happily took the seat next to him.

"Thanks for letting me sit with you guys. It's Lilou and Nico, right? Atlas told me about you. I hear you're siblings."

"Yep, that's right. Our mother, Adora, adopted all of us several years back, and we've been family ever since," Lilou replied, giving Atlas a warm smile.

An awkward pause followed; no one was sure what to say next. Lilou took it as an opportunity to ask questions. "Atlas says you've been here for a long time?"

"Yeah, almost a year. Hard to believe, right?" Mia replied. "You guys are probably wondering why I'm in here."

"Not just you. I want to know why all of these people are here," Atlas said.

"That's a difficult question to answer, as almost anything can land you in one of these prisons."

Nico gasped. *"One* of these prisons?"

"What? Did you guys think this was the only one? There are literally hundreds of prisons across the System," Mia explained.

"That can't be. What for?" Atlas asked in disbelief.

"For starters, you could be a refugee from one of the many realms completely overrun by P.O.R.T.A.L.," Mia said.

"Overrun by P.O.R.T.A.L.?" Nico echoed.

"Yeah, you know, like conquered or whatever."

Atlas said, "Last week, you asked me if I was a refugee from Earth C19. Can you tell us what happened there?"

"Sure. Earth C19 was a young realm at the height of its agricultural revolution. I don't know the full story, just bits and pieces I've been told. But from what I heard, one day out of the blue, P.O.R.T.A.L. showed up and started mining the realm's resources. They were supposedly searching for a rare element they believed could provide a new source of power for their war machine.

"They started enslaving the people, having them mine and extract the element. In one of the many revolts, a few brave people got their hands on a transponder, which they used to smuggle people out of C19. Anyone caught ended up in a place like this.

"See that table over there with the mom and her two children?" Mia asked, pointing to a table off in the corner. "Her name is Esme, and her two kids are

Armon and Kesi. They're refugees from Earth C19. They got here around the same time you guys did."

"That's all? That family was thrown in prison because they wanted to be free?" Lilou said angrily.

"It's sad, but that's just how things are, I guess. Let's see, what else? You could be a smuggler. That might be the most common reason; people who conduct illegal trade between realms. They smuggle all kinds of things, from weapons to drugs, from technology to information. Of course, the most serious reason that could land you here is treason," Mia said bluntly.

Atlas and Lilou gave her a blank stare.

"Treason ... you know, rebels — those fighting back against P.O.R.T.A.L. and the Council to free the Multiverse of tyranny kind of treason," Mia replied, almost mockingly.

"Wait, there are rebels out there?" Atlas asked.

"Duh, what do you think I'm in here for?" she said, her expression was serious.

Suddenly fearful of being watched by hidden surveillance, Atlas lowered his voice and whispered, "You're one of these rebels?"

Mia laughed. "Nah, I'm just kidding. Me? No way. Have you seen what they're up against? I'm just a small-time smuggler. And don't get too excited; I just smuggled food. Big market in the Multiverse for exotic foods. You guys should work with me if you ever get out. We can make a lot of money together."

Atlas ignored Mia's last comment and looked around the gymnasium, wondering which prisoners might be rebels. One prisoner across the gym made eye contact with him and nodded his head before raising his right hand and placing it across the center of his chest with his fingers spread wide. It was the same odd hand gesture that Atlas had seen the day he and Lilou and Nico got to the prison.

Atlas turned back to Mia. "What do you know about the Council? Who are these rebels fighting?"

"I know as much as anybody else I guess — which is nothing," she replied, now sounding almost bored.

"What do you mean, nothing? Who are they?" he persisted.

"Oh, you know. They just rule the known multiverse. Some believe the Council is one god-like being. Others believe it's a group of people. And some believe it was the original group of scientists who discovered the Multiverse; although the timeline never really made sense to me."

"How can nobody know who they are?" Lilou asked.

"They say only the top-ranking officers of P.O.R.T.A.L. know the truth about the Council. Maybe there is no Council. Maybe it's just a distraction, so nobody knows who the real enemy is. If you ask me, P.O.R.T.A.L. is the enemy. Destroy them, and the Council has nobody to do their dirty work," Mia replied.

Atlas leaned in closer, keeping his voice down. "How do we do that?" he said, intrigued by the prospect.

Mia laughed again. "Oh, we don't. I'm not a rebel, remember? Nobody can defeat P.O.R.T.A.L. They control everything. How do you defeat an enemy that can track your every movement?"

"How exactly can they track you?" Nico asked.

"They have an advanced system that monitors all the wormholes in the known multiverse. If a wormhole opens in one of their controlled realms, which they call the System, it sends them an alert. The only way to avoid detection is to use uncharted realms or black holes ... at least so I've heard," Mia explained.

Atlas looked confused. "Black holes?" he said.

"Wow, you guys really have a lot to learn about the Multiverse, don't you? Okay, so most wormholes are stable with small fluctuations. That's why P.O.R.T.A.L. doesn't know exactly where you'll come out. A black hole is completely unstable, meaning when you go in, there is no knowing where you'll end up. It's like playing roulette with the Multiverse. Black holes were once how they discovered all new realms. But now P.O.R.T.A.L. uses a sophisticated algorithm to predict where new realms will be. That's another reason why the rebels don't stand a chance."

Just then, the doors opened back up, signaling everyone to return to their cells. Lilou and Nico still had many questions about the Multiverse, but they'd have to wait until the next week. Lilou said, "It was really nice meeting you, Mia. Will you sit with us again next week?"

"Yeah, I'd like that," she replied.

Lilou and Nico stood and waved goodbye to Atlas and Mia before heading back to their cells.

"I guess we should walk back together?" Atlas asked, wondering if this was their routine now.

"Duh," was all Mia replied.

"Hey, Mia, you said that P.O.R.T.A.L. can track all wormholes; but my father says he's been working on a new transponder that would allow him to travel anywhere in the Multiverse. He says it will be more precise. Do you think P.O.R.T.A.L. will still be able to track him?" Atlas asked.

"That's impossible. Transponders only locate and use preexisting wormholes. What you're describing would mean creating a new wormhole. P.O.R.T.A.L.'s best scientists have been trying to do that unsuccessfully for decades. Who is your father, anyway? Some crazy scientist?" Mia looked skeptical.

"I don't know much about him, but I believe his name is Elio, and P.O.R.T.A.L. is looking for him. They called him *The Fugitive,*" Atlas replied

"Very funny. Elio is not your father," she replied, rolling her eyes.

"He is. That's why I'm here. My brother, sister, and I were looking for him before they captured us."

This time, it was Mia who stopped in her tracks. "Elio is your father? *The* Elio? The Father of the Rebellion?"

Atlas motioned for them to keep walking. "What do you mean, 'The Father of the Rebellion?'"

"Do I have to spell it out for you? He was the first rebel — the one who recruited the first realms to join the Outliers Alliance, the only free realms left in the known multiverse."

"I had no idea. He didn't tell me any of that," Atlas said, wondering why his father hadn't told him this.

"Of course he didn't tell you. No one has seen him for the past twelve years. Which is upsetting, because more realms are falling under the Council's rule every day," she said. "The Rebellion is practically over," she added, seeming unfazed.

Nobody has seen him? Why has he been hiding all these years? This revelation shocked Atlas. He knew his father was a fugitive and an enemy of

P.O.R.T.A.L., but until now, he'd had no idea to what extent he was involved.

Elio had told Atlas that he'd been sharing his technology with other realms, not that he was inciting a large-scale rebellion. It seemed the more Atlas learned, the less he knew who his father truly was; although the revelation that his father was a rebel made him more interested in reuniting with him.

"I wish we could talk longer. I'm really happy we met," Mia said, standing in front of her corridor. It was two corridors down from his on the opposite side.

"Yeah, me too. See you next week?"

"I'll still be here," she replied as she walked down the corridor toward her cell.

As Atlas watched her walk away, he realized that she was the first real friend he'd ever had, aside from his brother and sister. He saw her look back over her shoulder and give him a brief smile. Atlas smiled back, turned, and walked toward his cell.

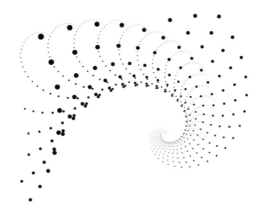

Chapter 8

Atlas spent the next week counting down the days, hours, and minutes until he would see Mia again. This time, instead of wondering when the door would slide open, he stood ready and waiting. When it did, he walked out and looked for her. He looked in front of her corridor where they had parted ways the week before, but no one was there. Figuring she must already be in the gymnasium, he hurried there.

He scanned the room and was upset not to find her. Instead, he found Lilou and Nico sitting together at their usual table. He took one last look around for Mia, then went over to his siblings. As he did, he felt a hand reach out, grab his arm, and pull him in the opposite direction. He whipped his head around to see who it was.

Surprised, yet relieved, he said, "Mia! Where have you been? I was looking for you." He wondered how he could have missed her.

"Don't worry about that now. We need to talk. Come with me," she said, pulling Atlas toward a corner table.

He took a seat. "Mia, what's going on? Is something wrong?"

"I have a plan to get us both out of here, but it won't be easy," she whispered, glancing around to make sure no one was watching.

"What do you mean, you have a plan? I thought this place was impossible to escape from?"

"Look, I haven't been completely honest with you. Remember when I said I was a smuggler? That wasn't entirely true," she said with a nervous smile.

"I don't understand."

"Just listen. I'm a spy. They sent me here to gather intelligence, but my mission is over, so it's time for me to leave, and I'm taking you with me."

"Mission? What mission?"

"The only mission: to find your father. We have spies looking for him across the Multiverse. As I told you, he's been missing for years. We suspected P.O.R.T.A.L. might have captured him. My mission was to pose as a smuggler, get captured, infiltrate this prison, and gather intelligence," she said matter-of-factly.

"I don't understand. When I told you about my father yesterday, you said the Rebellion didn't stand a chance," he said, looking perplexed.

"Trust me, when you told me who your father was, I wanted to believe you, but I had to be sure you were who you said you were. Luckily, we have a mole who works inside the prison. Last night I had him confirm that you are who you say you are. Apparently, you're big news with the soldiers. That's why I was late to the gym today. I was waiting for his confirmation."

"Confirmation? How do you even talk with him ... this ... mole?"

"Through the meal compartment, duh."

Atlas took a second to digest everything he'd just heard. *How is it that everyone in the Multiverse seems to be looking for the same man?* Although not entirely convinced, he asked the big question: "Okay, what's the plan?"

Mia gave Atlas a small, relieved smile. "Starting tomorrow," she said, "you're gonna fast for five days straight. Do you hear me? Five days." She held up five fingers spread wide. "You can drink water. In fact, you must, but do not eat anything; this will let our mole know exactly which cell you're in."

"Why five days?"

"Five is a symbolic number to the Rebellion. It represents the first five realms that formed the Outliers Alliance. Now listen carefully; on the sixth day you must eat everything. This will signal to our mole that you're not some random prisoner who is refusing their meals. Assuming the mole successfully picks up on your signal, on the seventh day, he'll replace your meal with a pill. You need to take that pill."

"What will the pill do to me?" he asked, concerned about where this was heading.

"Here's the thing. It will make you sick, very sick. It will give you a rare contagious and deadly disease, which has very ... let's say ... noticeable symptoms. Once P.O.R.T.A.L. catches wind that you're sick, they'll immediately remove you from the cellblock and quarantine you in the hospital ward. From there, I'm hoping they give you the cure," she said, her voice wavering a bit.

"Wait, time out. Your brilliant plan is for me to fast for five days, take a pill that will give me a deadly disease, and hope they give me the cure. What makes you think they'll give me a cure?"

"Keep your voice down. Listen, there are two ways out of this cellblock. You have to be dead or sick. Which do you prefer?" Mia asked rhetorically. "If you really are who you say you are, they'll keep you alive, because you're their best chance at finding Elio."

Atlas hesitated. He wanted to make sure he understood what was being asked of him. The only time he saw a soldier was when they brought a new prisoner into the cellblock, and he'd never seen a prisoner leave.

"Fine, I take the pill. I'm in the hospital ward, then what?" he said, keen to get to the actual escape.

"I don't know. That's as far as I've gotten," Mia replied.

"You don't know! What do you mean you don't know? It's your plan." It hit Atlas that there seemed to be a major flaw in the plan. "Wait, why am I taking the pill? You're the spy; you should take the pill," he whispered loudly.

Mia took a deep breath. Atlas thought she looked as though she'd run through this scenario many times in her head. "I can take the pill, and I will if you ask me to. But if they don't give me the cure, the mission is over, and nobody gets out. Remember, you're the only person in the prison of any value to P.O.R.T.A.L."

Atlas weighed the options and realized there was only one that would give them their best chance for success. "Okay, fine, I'll take the pill," he said reluctantly.

Mia gave Atlas a big smile of approval. "Good. Now, if it were me in that hospital ward, once I recovered, I'd escape by stealing one of the soldiers' handheld computers and opening our cellblocks," she said.

"Oh, I'm sorry. I didn't realize it was that simple," Atlas said sarcastically.

"Yep, that's it."

"What about Lilou and Nico?"

"That's why we need to time this perfectly. You need to open the exit door one week from today when the doors to the gym are open, and no prisoners are in their cells. That's the only way to rescue them."

Just then, the doors creaked open, signaling it was time for the prisoners to return to their cells.

Atlas whipped his head around to see if his siblings were still at their table; he needed to tell them about the plan. "Mia, I've got to go. I have to talk to my brother and sister." Without waiting for a response, he raced across the gymnasium.

"Lilou! Nico! I need to tell you something!" Atlas shouted before remembering that he should keep his voice down.

"There you are. I was wondering if you forgot about us. You didn't even come over to say hi. You and Mia really seem to get along," Lilou added, ignoring his comment.

Atlas lowered his voice. "Listen, I don't have time to explain everything. I have a plan to get us out of here." Atlas looked around. They were almost the last ones left in the room. "One week from today, you need to be ready."

"Did Mia come up with this plan?" Nico asked skeptically, looking over Atlas' shoulder to see if he could spot her.

"It doesn't matter right now. I just need you two to be ready, one week from *now,*" Atlas stressed.

Lilou sighed. "Okay, we'll be ready," she said, looking resigned to trusting her brother.

Atlas nodded his head, turned around, and strode toward the large steel door. As he approached it, the door started closing. He realized he'd have to run. He barely made it through the door and bumped into another prisoner on the other side. As he held her steady, he realized it was the refugee woman, Esme, with her two children, Armon and Kesi, the ones Mia explained had come from Earth C19. Esme was likely middle-aged but appeared older; her face was wrinkled and worn. Kesi looked around six or seven years old, and her brother Armon looked a few years younger. The blank, hopeless expressions on the children's faces reminded Atlas of the foster kids he grew up with.

"I'm sorry I bumped into you. I didn't mean to. I apologize," Atlas said.

Esme nodded her head. Though it appeared she was only pretending to know what he meant.

She can't understand me. Atlas looked at Armon and Kesi, and then back at her. Knowing Esme might not understand, he nonetheless whispered, "I'm going to get you out of here, I promise."

She nodded, smiled timidly, and started walking back to her cell.

He wondered if they shared a cell, or if they separated the children from her each week. He turned and ran back to his cell to mentally prepare himself for the days to come.

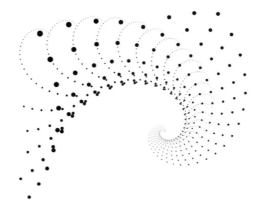

Chapter 9

Atlas woke up feeling anxious about the week to come. He wasn't completely confident in Mia's plan, but the rigid timeline left him little room for second guessing. Although his father had said he wouldn't be contacting him for another week, Atlas spent the better part of the morning lying on his cot, staring at the ceiling, desperately wishing to hear his father's voice reassure him that he was coming and there was no need to escape. That hope faded as the first meal of the day arrived.

As usual, it came from a small, motorized compartment at the back of the cell, next to the small sink, which was the only access to water. As soon as the compartment popped open and ejected his first tray of food, Atlas salivated at the thought of eating it. Since he'd had arrived in prison three weeks earlier, Atlas had been served two meals a day — one in the morning and one in the afternoon. Both consisted of one small pouch containing a light brown, slimy, grainy-liquid, which could be described as a form of gruel. It contained just enough sustenance to keep the prisoners alive. Although the gruel was practically tasteless, the realization that Atlas could not eat for the next five days made his craving even more pronounced.

Days one and two were the most challenging, because Atlas was unable to shake his desire for food. Drinking water to keep hydrated helped some, but not enough. Even more unbearable was the fact that he could see the food but couldn't eat it. By day three, Atlas had concluded that it was best to not even look at the food when it came out. He focused his attention elsewhere and waited until the food tray fully retracted into the wall before turning around. This could take as long as three to four hours. Atlas also battled intense headaches and nausea that made it difficult to concentrate.

He tried thinking about how he would complete his escape and always ended up wondering what he would do after he got to the hospital ward. Could he really escape the ward, steal a handheld computer, and open the cellblock, as Mia had urged? Growing up, Atlas had never even competed on the playground. He soon realized that it was pointless to think about the ward, since he had no idea what it looked like or how many doctors and soldiers he would encounter there.

By day four, as Atlas's digestive system started to shut down, his hunger subsided. To conserve energy, he spent most of the day lying on his back, adrift in his thoughts. Atlas recalled his last few conversations with Mia, trying to figure out if he'd missed any clues about her being a rebel spy. She did know an awful lot about the rebels, the Outliers Alliance, P.O.R.T.A.L., and the Council's ongoing battle for control of the Multiverse.

The thing that stuck out the most to him was how much she knew about his father, Elio. He couldn't say for sure it was a clue, because he had no idea how many people were aware of his father's name, but it did seem odd that Mia knew so much about a man who'd gone missing around the time she was born.

Perhaps the thing that might prove that she was, in fact, a rebel spy, was if her mole on the inside delivered the pill as promised. With ample time on his hands, Atlas thought a lot about the mole, and why that person might choose to help them escape. He concluded that the mole couldn't be a rebel, because then there would be no need for Mia to be in prison. His best guess was that the mole worked for P.O.R.T.A.L. but wanted to defect or was willing to help the rebels in exchange for money or something else of value.

On day five, Atlas could tell that his body had already started breaking down its fat reserves; he looked and felt significantly thinner. Simultaneously and inconveniently, he began having serious doubts about whether the plan would work, although perhaps his anxiety was just another symptom of starvation. Since he'd heard the plan, he'd thought little about what the pill would do to him. He knew it would make him sick, but how sick? He also vaguely remembered Mia saying something about the disease being rare and having "noticeable" symptoms. The more he replayed the conversation in his head, the more it frightened him.

Fortunately, he agreed with Mia's claim that if the doctors had the cure, they would save his life in hopes of finding his father. Yet even as he gained confidence, he couldn't help but question what made her so sure they had a cure for such a rare disease. As the day progressed, he managed to slowly push the negative thoughts out of his head. He did remember that on day six, he would be allowed to eat.

Day six finally arrived. Atlas woke up earlier than usual and waited for his first meal to appear. This was probably not a great decision, because the mere thought of food caused his stomach to ache. Nonetheless, he spent the morning staring at the back wall, waiting to hear the compartment door whir open and eject the food.

When it arrived, Atlas grabbed the pouch. He was about to gulp it down when he remembered something he'd learned years earlier in science class about starvation: his body would not be able to handle a full meal. So he slowly sipped on the pouch of gruel. After an hour, he started having stomach pains, even though he'd consumed only a quarter of the pouch.

Atlas felt frustrated. He'd waited five whole days to eat, and now the thing getting in his way was his own stomach. He tried to push through the pain but soon gave up. He put the pouch down and waited before trying to have more. Over the course of the day, he was able to finish most of his meal, but his stomach continued to ache. When the second pouch came, he couldn't even think about eating it. He resolved to save it for the next morning.

Waking up on the seventh day, Atlas was filled with a new sense of purpose. All week he'd been thinking about every last thing that could go wrong, at times losing sight of why he'd chosen to go through with the plan in the first place. He still felt guilty about bringing Lilou and Nico along without giving them a choice; he wanted the chance to make it right. He thought about Esme and her two children, to whom he'd made a promise. Finally, he remembered why he was here in the first place — to find his father and get the answers he desperately wanted.

Early that morning, he began to slowly sip on the pouch of gruel from the day before, still careful not to rush it into his system. After his drawn-out breakfast, he paced back and forth, waiting to see if the pill would replace the next meal. He got nervous that someone might be watching his odd behavior. He sat with his back against the plexiglass wall and stared at the meal compartment.

After what felt like hours, the compartment opened and ejected the first meal tray. From his vantage point on the floor, Atlas saw that the tray was empty. To confirm if there was indeed a pill on it, he was forced to stand. He inched his way toward the tray. When he was right above it, he nearly missed the little red pill lying there. It was much smaller than he'd expected. He crouched, picked it up with his thumb and index finger and brought it close to his face to examine. Then he carefully placed it on his tongue and swallowed it.

The pill was so small he felt around his mouth with his tongue to confirm it had gone down his throat. Coming up empty, he was left with nothing but time and silence to wonder exactly how long it would take before the symptoms would kick in.

After what felt like an hour of standing in nervous anticipation, Atlas gave himself permission to lie on his cot. He wondered if anything was going to happen at all. As his mind drifted, the first symptom appeared: He felt as though he was coming down with a fever. His forehead and hands began to sweat profusely. Although the fever seemed quite high and the sweating was uncomfortable, Atlas thought for an optimistic minute that it might not be too bad as long as he didn't start vomiting. That thought soon faded, because his feet and legs began swelling up like balloons. The swelling spread up his body, through his abdomen, chest, and neck.

Looking down, his body was unrecognizable. Sadly, the swelling advanced to his lips, cheeks, and eyes, eventually sealing his mouth shut and distorting his vision. Finally, his breathing became increasingly labored as his throat swelled. At this moment, Atlas wondered if the doctors would reach him in time.

Atlas wasn't sure how long he'd been lying face down on the floor, barely breathing, when he heard the plexiglass door slide open, followed by two unfamiliar voices.

"What do we have here?" said a man, who was obviously looking at Atlas's motionless body.

"Is he dead?" a second man asked. He didn't sound overly concerned.

"I sure hope not. The boss wouldn't be pleased. I guess there's only one way to find out. Here, grab his legs. I'll grab his arms, and we can get him up on this gurney," the first man replied.

Atlas felt himself being lifted onto the gurney. It was still extremely difficult to breathe because of the swelling in his throat. His eyes had almost swelled shut, making it hard to see anything. All he could make out through his eyelids were two blurry black figures. He guessed they were soldiers.

"Ehh —what's wrong with his face?" one of them asked, sounding disgusted.

"Is he even breathing?" the other one said.

"Yeah, look right there. I think I see his chest moving."

"I guess that means we better get him down to the hospital ward as directed."

Atlas felt the gurney move down the hall. "You know, I don't understand why we're even bothering to help this scum. He looks disposable if you ask me."

"You know exactly why; Allister Craum wants him alive. Word around the prison is his father is someone of *importance.*"

Atlas heard what sounded like one of the soldiers pushing buttons on a handheld device to open the prison block's door.

"Allister Craum — I can't stand him and his pointed little nose. Ever since he got promoted, he walks around like he runs the place." The soldier sounded annoyed.

"He does run the place, dummy," the other soldier reminded him as they pushed the gurney down a corridor.

"Well, as soon as I get promoted, I'm going to ask to be transferred to Earth AII, so I don't have to take orders from Cranky Craum anymore. Plus, my brother, who's stationed there, said that the women are the most beautiful in the entire System."

"First, you are never getting promoted. Second, I've explained this to you a million times — they have the same women on Earth AII as we do here; it's just an alternate realm with a bunch of doppelgangers."

"Yeah, I know. But they dress better." The gurney stopped.

"Just ring the doorbell, would you?"

"This is Dr. Owen. What do you need?" a voice called through the intercom.

"We have the prisoner from Cellblock A. Allister Craum ordered us to bring him to you immediately."

"All right, bring him in," the doctor replied.

Atlas heard the door buzz and felt himself being pushed into a brightly lit room.

"Oh my goodness," the doctor said, "how long has he been like this?"

"I don't know, a few hours maybe. Someone watching the monitors noticed him lying still. They sent us in to bring him down here."

"I need to act fast. Help me move him onto that bed," the doctor ordered.

They lifted Atlas by his arms and legs and placed him on a hospital bed.

"This is strange, very strange indeed. Do either of you know what realm this prisoner is from?"

Neither soldier responded to his question. Finally, one of them asked, "Is something wrong?" as they watched the doctor frantically searched through cabinets with vials that jingled as he moved them around.

"Yes, something is wrong, very wrong. This patient appears to be suffering from *Morbius Inflatorium,* an extremely rare and deadly disease found in only one known realm. I haven't encountered this in decades; it was thought to be eradicated," the doctor explained.

Morbius Inflatorium? Atlas thought, lying on his back, listening to the conversation. *Eradicated ...?*

"Well, if there's nothing else we can do to help, we should head back to our posts now," one of the soldiers said.

"Oh, no-no-no. You two can't leave yet. This disease is contagious, and you've both been exposed. Take off all your clothes and put them in that hazardous materials bag to be sanitized. You can change into the scrubs hanging on the wall. Then go straight back to your living quarters, scrub down thoroughly, and quarantine yourselves in your bunks until further notice. Do you understand?"

The soldiers stood still, apparently not grasping the seriousness of the situation. After a few long seconds, one said to the other, "I guess that means we are off duty for a couple of weeks, huh?"

"Yeah, thanks Doc!" the other one exclaimed.

Atlas could hear the two strip down, put on the scrubs, and open the door.

The doctor said, "Oh, no. You need to leave *everything.*"

"You want me to leave my computer? I don't think so," the soldier said.

"I'll have it sanitized and delivered to your bunk within the hour; I promise. Or you can take it, but when there's an outbreak in the facility, I'm going to have to explain to Allister Craum that I instructed you to leave it here and how you willfully disobeyed my instructions."

"Fine," the soldier responded in an annoyed tone. Atlas heard him place the computer on the countertop and walk out.

Atlas tried to replay every detail of the conversation, but he couldn't. His breathing continued to worsen, and his vision faded.

He barely heard the doctor say, "Ah, here it is. You, young man, are in need of this." The doctor had apparently found the medicine he needed. "This will only hurt a bit," the doctor assured Atlas, as he stuck a needle in his arm. "And one more for good measure," he said, delivering a second shot into Atlas's other arm.

"There. You should feel yourself recovering quickly now. The first shot was the vaccine, which should eradicate the disease, and the second shot should help reduce the swelling, though it may take a few hours before it's completely gone."

Almost immediately, Atlas felt the swelling in his throat subside, and his breathing return to normal. Soon, he saw more clearly as the swelling in his eyes decreased. When his eyesight was fully restored, he glanced to his left. The doctor, his back toward Atlas, was reorganizing the vials in his cabinet.

Atlas's heartbeat increased; it was time to act. He spotted the soldier's handheld computer on the counter near the exit door. He had to find a way to get past the doctor, grab the computer, and get to the cellblock to release Mia, Lilou, and Nico so they could all escape.

Trying desperately not to make a sound, Atlas slowly sat up and placed his feet softly on the ground. A small tray table with a set of instruments was on his right, next to his bed. One of the tools appeared bulky and heavy. Atlas grabbed it, stood, and inched his way toward the doctor, who hadn't noticed he was mobile. He raised the instrument over his shoulder, ready to bring it down forcefully on the doctor's head, when the doctor said mildly, "What are you doing, young man? Were you really going to hit me over the head with that after I just cured you?"

Atlas, who wasn't sure if he could speak, stood frozen in disbelief.

"Well, aren't you going to say anything?"

Atlas now felt terrible for wanting to bash the doctor over the head. "I'm sorry," he said.

"Very good. Now if I were you, I'd go over there, pull one of the uniforms from that bag, put it on, grab the computer lying on the counter, and go rescue your little friends. That's what you're here for, yes?"

It took Atlas a second to register all this. Once he did, he opened his mouth and said, "You're the mole."

"Precisely. You're smarter than you look. Now, what are you waiting for?" the doctor asked, motioning to the bag.

Atlas put down the instrument and went over to the bag containing the uniforms. Before he grabbed one, he stopped. "I don't understand. Why are you helping me?" he said.

"Because, young man, we're all prisoners here. P.O.R.T.A.L. needs doctors, and doctors are not exactly jumping at the opportunity to work for P.O.R.T.A.L., so they kidnap them, separate them from their families, and force them to work in places like this," he said dolefully, glancing at a family picture hanging on the wall.

"But the pill. Mia. How did you ...?"

"I treated Mia when she was first brought here. I suspected that she might be a rebel. So one day, I paid one of the kitchen workers to send her a note through the meal compartment. We've been in contact ever since. When she told me there was someone she needed to get out, I came up with the idea for the pill. Who else do you think would have access to such a deadly disease and its cure?"

"But why didn't Mia take the pill? You would have given her the cure, the same as me," Atlas said.

"That was my original plan, but Mia said she had to make sure you were serious about escaping. She needed to know if you had it in you," the doctor explained.

She needed to know that I had it in me?

"I thought it was a risky move myself, but here we are. Now go, before Allister Craum comes looking for you," the doctor said, his tone urgent.

Atlas took out one of the uniforms and put it on over his jumpsuit. Luckily, his height came in handy; the adult-size uniform fit him perfectly. Once dressed, he grabbed the computer and reached for the door handle. He turned to face the doctor one last time. "Won't you get in trouble for this?" he asked, worried.

"Don't fret about me. Once you leave, I'm going to give myself a heavy sedative. When they eventually find me passed out, I'll wake up and act like I don't remember a thing," he said with a smile. "What about cameras? You said you were a prisoner yourself. Aren't they watching you?"

"Don't worry. There are no cameras in here for the same reason there are no guards in your cellblock. P.O.R.T.A.L. isn't worried about me escaping. In exchange for my work here, P.O.R.T.A.L. leaves my family alone. As long as that's the arrangement, they know I'm not going anywhere.

"Now, listen. Once you leave this room, walk down the corridor to your left. When you reach the end of that corridor, turn right, then it's a straight walk to the prison block. Be aware, there may be no cameras in here, but once outside that door, there are cameras everywhere. You need to walk and act like a soldier — and keep your head down."

"Thank you," was all Atlas could muster. He stood and left the hospital ward in a soldier's uniform and computer in hand.

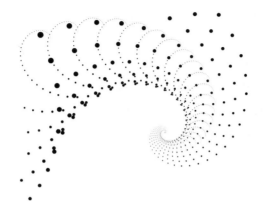

Chapter 10

Atlas turned left down the corridor and started jogging when he remembered the doctor's warning about the cameras. He transitioned quickly into his best impression of a soldier marching, keeping his shoulders back and taking even strides. At the end of the corridor, he turned right, as instructed. The corridor curved to the left. Once around the bend, he saw a large door with a sign above it that read Cellblock A. As Atlas walked toward the door, he passed an adjacent corridor where two soldiers were patrolling. Luckily, they were walking away from him, so he continued toward the door. He pulled out the handheld computer and tapped the screen. It lit up and was filled with dozens of small, unfamiliar icons. Atlas scanned through them until he found one labeled Building Schematics. As he clicked on it, he heard a voice coming from the corridor to his right.

"You there. What are you doing? Why are you not at your post?"

Atlas ignored the voice as he searched for the door's key code. A blueprint of the building presented itself and automatically displayed the floor he was on. From there, he figured he just needed to find the door labeled Cellblock A.

"Hey, I'm talking to you! It's gymnasium day. You can't go in there. The prisoners aren't in their cells!" the voice called out.

Atlas scrolled through the map, searching for any thing labeled Cellblock A. He came across a word he'd heard Allister Craum use in the interrogation room. There on the map was a large room labeled Purgatory. He hesitated, wondering what it was used for, but with no time to ponder, he continued his search for Mia and his siblings.

Fortunately, the soldier was still a ways down the hall when Atlas found the right door. He pressed the image of the door, and to his pleasant surprise, the big door in front of him slid open.

Atlas took one last glance at the approaching soldier, then raced through the open door. On the other side, he sprinted toward the gymnasium. From behind, he heard the soldier frantically yelling, "Get back here!"

As he ran, he pressed the image of the door again, locking it behind him. *Great, I'm back inside the prison,* he thought. Up ahead, he saw the backs of prisoners on their way to the gymnasium. Some turned to see who was running toward them. They gave Atlas puzzled looks. Their calm but quizzical expressions showed that they recognized him but were confused by his soldier's uniform. He pushed his way through the crowd, yelling, "Mia! Mia! I'm here!" He saw her up ahead, moving through the crowd in his direction.

When they were close, Mia exclaimed, "Atlas, you did it! You got it."

"Yes, but someone saw me. There are soldiers outside the door. They'll be here any second. What are we going to do?" he asked, wondering how their situation now was any better than before.

"Don't worry about them. You get your brother and sister. I'll handle the soldiers," Mia said.

Atlas was about to question her, but she was already heading toward the exit. A couple prisoners, who had overheard their conversation, followed her. He turned and continued to push through the prisoners to get to the gymnasium. Through the open door, he saw Lilou and Nico running in his direction. They clearly remembered what he'd told them about being ready.

When they reached him just outside the door, Lilou started in on him. "Atlas, what's happening? Why are you wearing a soldier's uniform? What's wrong with your face?" she asked in quick succession.

"I don't have time to explain, but we need to go. This computer can open the exit door, but there are soldiers waiting for us," Atlas replied, still unsure how they would actually escape.

"Where's Mia?" Nico asked. "I know she must be involved."

"She's at the exit. Come on, follow me," Atlas replied, turning, and running back toward Mia.

A small number of the prisoners around them who hadn't yet entered the gymnasium caught on that something was happening. They followed Atlas back toward the entrance. When Atlas, Lilou, and Nico and their followers turned the corner to the main corridor that led to the cellblock's exit door, they were cheered by the unexpected sight of Mia crouched on top of a soldier, delivering a knockout punch. Their eyes were then drawn to five other lifeless bodies scattered about the corridor floor. Standing above two of those bodies were two prisoners who appeared to have helped Mia in the melee.

"What happened here?" Atlas asked.

"I'm starting to really like your girlfriend," Lilou said.

Girlfriend? Atlas thought.

Mia looked up at them. "We need to move," she said. She picked up one of the soldier's rifles and slung it over her shoulder.

A few of the more capable prisoners who had followed them caught on that there was a mutiny in progress. They grabbed the remaining rifles off the floor.

The escapees — Atlas, Mia, Lilou, Nico, and a handful of prisoners, were racing toward the exit when a new squadron of soldiers entered the prison block, firing bright energy pulses from their rifles. The siblings and Mia ducked into one of the prison cells in time to dodge the pulses, as a battle between prisoners and soldiers ensued in the cellblock corridor.

"Keep your heads down!" Mia shouted as she darted in and out of the cell to return fire.

"What do we do now?" Atlas asked. "That was the only exit."

Speaking in a hushed tone, Nico said, "That can't be the only exit."

Lilou heard this. "You said yourself that was the only exit," she reminded him.

"Atlas, give me that computer," Nico directed. "There has to be more than one way in and out of this place."

"Can you three speed it up? I can't hold them back much longer!" Mia yelled as she ducked just in time to dodge another energy pulse.

Nico swiped through the computer icons until he came across the building schematics map Atlas had found earlier. His eyes lit up. "I think I may have found something. This is where we are, and that's the exit guarded by those soldiers. But look here," he said pointing, "back in the gym, on the floor, there's something labeled Maintenance Hatch." He held up the computer for Atlas and Lilou to see.

Lilou frowned. "I never saw a maintenance hatch in the gym."

"I haven't seen one either, but it's on the map. It has to be there," Nico responded.

Newly hopeful, Atlas said, "There's only one way to find out. We need to get back to the gym."

"Back to the gym?" Mia said, having heard only the last part of the plan. "You guys better know something I don't."

"Just trust us," Atlas said.

"Fine, get behind me. I'll lay down cover fire."

The siblings crouched behind Mia and waited for her signal. She took a deep breath, exhaled, then jumped into the middle of the corridor and started firing wildly at the soldiers, forcing them to take cover. Atlas, Lilou, and Nico took that as a signal to run for the gym.

On their way, they passed two prisoners: the ones who had helped Mia. One was a tall and muscular man with a thick greying mustache. The other was a shorter, skinnier, and bald-headed man with a dark goatee. The two prisoners ran toward the soldiers' position firing their rifles. This allowed Mia to retreat with the others. The four of them ran down the corridor toward the gymnasium.

Atlas shouted, "Nico! Press the image of the Gymnasium Door and it will open."

Nico did, and they waited anxiously until the door opened slowly in front of them. Once they were inside, a crowd of scared prisoners, who must have heard the shooting, confronted them.

"Nico, where's this exit?" Atlas asked, feeling pressured.

"According to the map, it's in the center of the gym."

"Come on. We need to find it, *now!*"

They ran to the center of the gymnasium. Nico pulled up the building's schematic screen and pressed the Maintenance Hatch icon. Immediately, a circle on the floor in front of them slid open, revealing a ladder leading down to a dark space.

Mia shouted, "What are you guys staring at? Let's get out of here!" She began climbing down the ladder.

Just then, the two helpful prisoners from the cellblock came running back through the gymnasium door.

Lilou said, "Where are the rest?"

"They didn't make it. More soldiers are coming," explained the taller prisoner. "I sure hope you have a way out."

"We need to go," Atlas mumbled, just loud enough for Lilou to hear.

"Atlas, what about the rest of the prisoners?" she said, looking at all the scared faces around them.

Atlas realized they were looking for guidance. "We take anyone who wants to come," he whispered to Lilou.

Atlas stepped forward. "We're getting out of here. If anyone wants to come, follow us down that ladder," he said. Most of the prisoners remained where they were, looking frightened, but a few stepped out of the crowd and joined the rifle-wielding prisoners near the open hatch.

Atlas suddenly remembered Esme, Armon, and Kesi. Scanning the crowd, he spotted them nearby. He rushed over to her. "Come with us," he said, holding out his hand. Although she looked fearful, she nodded and took his hand. Her children clutched her other hand. They ran back to the hatch and followed Lilou and Nico, who were part way down the ladder.

When Atlas reached the bottom with Esme and her children, he found his siblings, Mia, and about a dozen prisoners. "This is it? This is everyone who chose to come?" he said.

"Nico, close the hatch!" Mia shouted. She kicked the ladder several times, causing it to break and fall. Nico pressed the Maintenance Hatch icon, and they watched as the hatch above them slid soundly shut. They assumed the soldiers chasing them would also have access to the hatch, but they hoped the soldiers would search the rest of the prison first, giving them the head start they needed.

They found themselves standing at the center of a hub of passageways that extended out in all directions. They saw electrical boxes along the wall of the hub and what looked like piping and wiring leading into the passageways. Although the hub was large and well lit, the passageways they'd have to navigate looked dark and narrow.

"What is this place?" Atlas asked. He took off his soldier's uniform and threw it aside.

"They must use these passageways to maintain and service the building," Nico replied.

"But which way do we go?" Lilou said, looking at the many passageways.

Mia said, "We need to get to the main flight deck. We're going to fly out of here."

The bigger and more intimidating prisoner stepped forward. "Wait a second, who put the kids in charge?"

His shorter companion, who was standing next to him, added, "Yeah, he's right. They look like they're in middle school."

"If it weren't for us kids, you two would still be up there, remember?" Mia said.

"It was us who saved your butt back in that corridor, remember?" he retorted. "And if you're going to fly out of here, you're going to need a pilot," he added.

"And let me guess, you're a pilot?"

"That's right, you're looking at the best smuggler in the Multiverse," he said, looking around for recognition but receiving none.

"If you're so good, what are you doing here?" Mia retorted.

"I could ask you the same thing, sweetheart," the prisoner quipped back.

"Touche. Congratulations, you got the job. And don't call me sweetheart. My name's Mia. What about you? Got a name, co-pilot? Or should I just call you Ogre?"

"Very funny. The name's Frank, and this is my partner, Stew."

"Perfect. Now can we please go?"

Atlas realized, despite considering Mia a friend and ally, he knew virtually nothing about her past. He shook off that thought and said to Nico, "Can you get us to the flight deck?"

"These passageways aren't on the building's schematics, but I imagine if we head in that direction, I can get us there," Nico replied, confidently.

The group followed Nico down the passageway he'd indicated. Armon and Kesi had a hard time keeping up, so Atlas and Lilou each grabbed one of them by the hand. When they arrived at the next hub, Nico stopped, looked at the computer, and checked to see which way they needed to go. They followed him from hub to hub, making slight adjustments to their course until they got close to the flight deck.

"It's just up ahead," Nico told them. "It looks like there's another maintenance hatch. When we can get there, I'll open it. That should bring us right onto the flight deck."

As they headed toward the final hub, Atlas heard his father's voice.

Atlas, my child, can you hear me? I have returned.

Atlas stopped and looked at Lilou. "Lilou, take her, I need to check something," Atlas directed, handing Kesi off to Lilou.

"Atlas, what's wrong?"

"It's nothing, I'll be right behind you. I promise."

Lilou took both children by the hand and hurried to catch up with the others.

Atlas let Lilou and the group get slightly ahead of him. "Yes, I can hear you," he replied, using his internal voice.

I have good news. I have made progression on my ...

Atlas cut him off. "Father, there's no time for that. We're in the middle of escaping."

Escaping? How?

"We got help from someone on the inside. I'll explain everything later, but now we need your help. We're almost out of the prison. Where is your portal?" Atlas asked, knowing his father was somewhere outside of the city.

Atlas, I want to help, but I need to know who will be with you.

"It doesn't matter. There's no time to explain, we'll be there soon. Where is your portal?" Atlas repeated urgently.

Okay ... once you're out of the city, head east until you see a lake. I'm on the south bank of that lake, above the dam. But remember, you have little time. They're tracking me.

"Then I guess I'll see you in eight minutes," Atlas said, knowing it would take P.O.R.T.A.L. that long to track his father's wormhole.

Atlas rushed to catch up to the group. "Nico! Open that hatch. We need to go, *now!*"

"I'm already on it," Nico replied. The group took a step back as the floor above them slid open, just as it had in the gymnasium.

"Someone needs to go up first and make sure the coast is clear," Mia said. She let her eyes linger on Frank and Stew to see if one of them would step up.

Stew snorted. "What are you looking at us for? I'm not going up first."

"Fine, I'll do it," Mia said, grabbing the ladder and climbing up.

Lilou and the children stood next to Atlas at the bottom of the ladder. "How does she even know how to fly one of those ships, anyway? She's like the same age as us," Lilou said.

"I have no idea," Atlas replied, his eyes glued to the open hatch. "But we're gonna have to trust her and we need to move fast."

Moments later, Mia poked her head out in the opening and waved for the rest of the group to follow.

Atlas turned to Lilou and Nico. "You two take Armon and Kesi and go up first." They each helped one child climb the ladder. He then turned to Esme. "We'll keep them safe, I promise," he said, before motioning her to follow Lilou and Nico up the ladder next.

Atlas continued to send the rest of the prisoners up the ladder ahead of him. Once they were all up top, he looked to ensure no one was left behind, then made his own way up. As he poked his head through the hatch's opening, he heard shooting. Mia and Stew were standing on a transport ship's cargo ramp returning fire to a small group of soldiers in the distance while somehow also ushering the prisoners on board.

Mia saw Atlas and shouted, "Atlas, get on board!"

He climbed out of the hatch and ran toward the ship while dodging energy pulses at his feet. As he ran up the cargo ramp, he heard Mia scream.

He turned and saw her lying on the ramp, holding her right arm with her left hand, yet continuing to fire her rifle with the injured arm.

Atlas looked up and saw the man in the white suit, who he now knew was Allister Craum, casually standing behind his soldiers, giving them orders. Atlas and one of the prisoners who had been returning fire grabbed Mia under her arms and dragged her up the cargo ramp. She reached out and hit a button with her fist, closing the ramp.

"Are you okay?" Atlas asked, looking at her wounded arm.

"I'll be fine. It barely grazed me. Just help me stand," Mia replied calmly.

Once on her feet, she walked past the passengers in the cargo hold and into the cockpit, still holding her wound. Atlas followed. Frank was in the co-pilot seat, and Lilou and Nico were sitting in the row of seats behind him.

"Prime the ignition," she ordered Frank.

"It's already done," he replied.

"I'm impressed. I guess you're not so useless after all," Mia said. She sat in the pilot's seat and started pushing buttons on the ship's control panels. "You, Stew, and I are making quite the team; aren't we?"

"Don't get ahead of yourself," he said. "Just fly this ship out of here."

Atlas watched in amazement before taking the last open seat behind Mia. The engine began to hum, and the ship lifted off the ground and hovered in place.

"Nico, the door!" Mia shouted.

Nico used the computer to open the building's giant hangar door. As the ship moved toward the opening, they felt the vessel vibrate and shake from ongoing fire from the soldiers on the ground.

When the hangar was fully open, Mia pushed the throttle forward, and they flew into the city beyond, speeding up to ascend high above the skyscrapers and away from danger.

Atlas stood and leaned over Mia's seat. "Mia, we need to head east."

"East? Why? We just need to get as far away from P.O.R.T.A.L. as possible."

"It's my father. He will be there, on the south bank of a lake, behind the dam." Atlas said, hoping he wouldn't have to elaborate.

"Your father? How do you know?"

"I can't explain, but he will be there. You have to trust me."

Mia paused, then took a hard left, causing everyone on board to brace themselves. Once the ship was headed in the right direction, it took only a minute before they saw the lake in the distance.

"Did you say your father is going to be there?" Lilou asked.

"Yes. Just before we boarded, he contacted me and said he'd be waiting for us," Atlas replied, knowing this was only partially true.

As they neared the lake, Mia started their descent. As they got closer to the water's edge, they saw what appeared to be a portal and a man standing on the shore frantically waving his arms. Mia gently brought the ship down and landed on the lakeshore, twenty yards from the man.

Atlas tried to catch a glimpse of his father through the cockpit window, but Mia had landed the ship facing away from the portal.

The siblings and Mia rushed to the back of the ship and opened the cargo hold. Lilou and Nico helped the prisoners off and pointed them in the portal's direction before assisting Esme and her children. Then they headed to the portal themselves.

Atlas stood on the cargo ramp and determined that everyone was safely off the ship before following Lilou and Nico.

At the portal, Atlas heard Lilou whisper to Nico, "Come on, let's give Atlas and his father some space," before walking side-by-side through the rift.

Elio held out his arms. "Atlas, my son, after all these years, I have finally found you."

Atlas stood stock-still, staring at his father. He looked just like he had in the picture, with his facial hair, full beard, long hair, and reading glasses. Although Atlas had never seen Elio in person, his father's eyes looked familiar. Elio was wearing what looked like a dirty old robe, worn tan pants, and big sun hat. He indeed looked like a man who'd been on the run for twelve years.

Atlas wanted to say something, but couldn't find any words, so he stepped forward and hugged his father. He couldn't pinpoint the emotions he was feeling. Growing up as an orphan and moving from foster home to foster home had taught him to be wary of new relationships — because they rarely lasted.

Elio looked over Atlas's shoulder. P.O.R.T.A.L. ships were approaching in the distance. He said, "It's time for us to go, my son." He wrapped his arm around Atlas's shoulders and guided him into the wormhole.

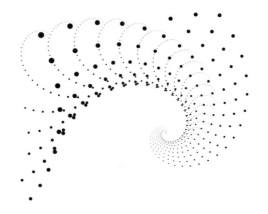

Chapter 11

When they emerged on the other side, Elio closed the portal behind them. Atlas found himself standing on a small island surrounded by water. In every direction he looked, he saw more islands. They seemed to be in the middle of nowhere, far from civilization. Up ahead, Lilou, Nico, and Mia were standing with the group of freed prisoners on the sand by the water. Atlas turned to his father. "Where are we?"

"This is nowhere of importance. It's an uncharted realm outside the known multiverse. But this is not our final destination. I learned many years ago that the best way to avoid detection from P.O.R.T.A.L. is to do what I refer to as realm-hopping," Elio explained.

"Realm-hopping?"

"Yes. I never travel directly to any realm that is part of the System. I always travel to an uncharted realm first. That way, if P.O.R.T.A.L. detects my wormhole and tries to follow me, they will end up in a place such as this."

"Then where is our final destination?"

"Ah, you will see. But first, let's get these innocent people home."

Elio joined the crowd on the beach, who formed a circle around him. Some of them clearly recognized Elio; all of them waited for him to speak. "I know where you've all come from, and what you've been through. No one should ever have to endure that kind of pain and suffering, but today you get to go home to your families. Before you go, you must understand that the Council will not rest until they have control of the entire multiverse. Please remember this moment when the call comes to join your brethren in the fight against P.O.R.T.A.L. and the Council."

Elio turned on his transponder, and the holographic map of the Multiverse appeared. "If you know your destination, step forward and enter the coordinates into this transponder. If you do not know your destination or don't feel safe returning home, I will open a wormhole to Earth A27. This will take you to a refuge controlled by the Outliers Alliance. You will find allies there waiting to assist you."

Out of the dozen prisoners in the circle, only four approached Elio to enter their coordinates. The remaining prisoners, including Frank, Stew, Esme, and her children, waited for Elio to open the wormhole that would take them to Earth A27.

Once the wormhole opened, Frank stepped forward and said, "Nice flying back there, kiddo."

"You weren't so bad yourself," Mia replied.

And one by one they left, leaving the siblings and Mia with Elio.

"Now that's done; it's time for me to show you my home," Elio said. He opened another wormhole. "Please, after you." The four gave each other a knowing glance and stepped through the portal together.

On the other side, they found themselves on a mountainside, surrounded by massive evergreen trees, and standing in a cold wind. Through the tree line in front of them, the mountain range extended out in all directions. A moment later, Elio joined them and closed the wormhole.

"Well, I think introductions are in order, but first, let's go inside, shall we?" he said. He walked up the mountain toward a small cabin half hidden in the trees.

The four watched him walk off but stayed put, taking a moment for themselves. In a voice filled with pride, Lilou said, "Atlas, you've done it, you found your father!"

"*We* found him," Atlas corrected her.

Since their arrival, Mia had been quiet. Atlas said, "Mia, thank you for all your help, we couldn't have done it without you."

"Hey, you were the one who took the pill, remember? I knew you could do it," she said with a smile, still holding her wounded right arm.

Atlas took a deep breath. "I guess it's time to find out who my father is," he said, walking toward the cabin.

Lilou and Mia followed him, but Nico remained where he was. "Wait, you guys haven't noticed?" he called after them.

Atlas stopped. "Noticed what?"

"Who your father is," Nico said.

Lilou looked perplexed. "What are you talking about? We've never met him before."

"Yes, that's technically correct, but ..."

Atlas cut him off. "Dr. Faraday ... he's talking about Dr. Faraday," Atlas said, almost to himself. He now knew where he'd seen his father's eyes before.

Elio's shape, beard, hair, and glasses had concealed his identity.

Lilou said, "Now I'm really confused."

"From what I've gathered," Nico told them, "the Multiverse is made up of billions of earths with infinite possibilities. That means there is more than one Elio in the Multiverse. In our realm, he's called Malcolm Faraday."

Lilou's eyes opened wide. "That would mean there is more than one of us, right?"

"Yes, that's correct," Nico said, having already figured this out.

"That's pretty amazing," Lilou said. "But if you haven't noticed, it's beginning to snow and I'm freezing my butt off. Can we please go inside and talk about it there?"

The cabin was one large room. Elio was filling a kettle in a small kitchen in the back corner. To their right, a small table was set with tea mugs. To their left, a coffee table that seated six was surrounded by a few small sofas. In the center of the room a wooden ladder was attached to the front of a loft that covered the entire back of the cabin.

Elio turned to greet them. "Oh good, you made it. I was wondering when you were going to come out of that cold. Please, have a seat by the fire. I'm just boiling water for tea."

The four seated themselves on the sofa. Elio soon joined them and offered them tea. When none of them took him up on his offer, Elio began.

"Which ones are your brother and sister?" he asked Atlas, seeing more guests than he'd expected.

"This is Lilou, and this is Nico; they're my siblings. And this is my friend Mia. She's the one who helped us escape. She was also looking for you," Atlas explained.

"Looking for me, huh? Now why would you be doing that, young lady?"

Mia leaned forward and crossed her arms. "You either don't know what's happened since you left, or you don't care. I saw you talking to those prisoners as if there's a glimmer of hope left. Well, there isn't. The Rebellion is lost. My father trusted you, he believed in you, and he died fighting for your cause, leaving me and my mother to fend for ourselves."

The siblings looked at each other nervously, realizing there was more to Mia's story than they'd known.

"I am sorry to hear about your loss, child, I truly am. And I'm sorry about what has happened to the Rebellion since I left. But you must understand, we were losing the war. For every realm I freed, P.O.R.T.A.L. controlled a dozen more. They've always had the upperhand.

"Remember, you are not the only one who sacrificed something for this war. I lost my wife, and I was forced to abandon my unborn child. After that, I realized the only way to defeat them was not through force, but through my technology. That's why I've spent the last twelve years trying to develop a new transponder that will give *us* the upper hand. When it's complete, the Rebellion will be restored, and we will be able to take back control of the Multiverse," Elio said earnestly.

"I'm sorry, but that's not good enough. You gave up. My father didn't," Mia said. She stood and walked to the back of the room; her shoulders hunched.

"It's not like that, child. I never gave up, there is more to the story," Elio said, but Mia kept her back turned to them.

Atlas broke the silence that followed. "What do you mean you 'were forced' to abandon me. What happened to you that night?"

"Atlas, this isn't how I envisioned telling you this story, but if I must." Elio took a big sip of his tea, stood, and paced. "Many years ago, with the help of my trusted partner, I developed the technology that allowed for interdimensional travel between realms. I was praised and celebrated for my discovery. But not long after, P.O.R.T.A.L. discovered our realm and demanded that we turn over the technology and kneel before the Council's rule. Our realm tried to fight back, but how can you fight against a force with endless resources? During the final battle for control of our realm, my partner and I made a narrow escape.

"After the devastating loss, we felt personally responsible for what had happened to our realm. We took a vow to never stop resisting P.O.R.T.A.L. and the Council until our realm was once again free. We traveled the Multiverse together. We visited realms as yet undiscovered, to share our technology with them and warn them. We hoped our technology would give them a fighting chance once P.O.R.T.A.L. arrived.

"During our journey, we met a brilliant young scientist set on making a name for himself as an inventor. I took him under my wing as my apprentice and taught him everything I knew about the Multiverse and interdimensional travel. The three of us set out on a quest to free the Multiverse.

"For many years, we stayed one step ahead of P.O.R.T.A.L. And together we formed the Outliers Alliance: five realms that vowed never to kneel to the Council's rule. Soon, the Alliance grew to include dozens of realms, and the war for control of the Multiverse began. The war raged on for years, with heavy casualties on both sides. Through many battles and dangerous journeys together, my trusted partner — your mother — and I fell deeply in love.

"But the tide turned when P.O.R.T.A.L. developed an algorithm that allowed them to discover new realms at an accelerated pace. Soon, every advanced realm we stumbled upon was already controlled by P.O.R.T.A.L., marking the turning point in the war and the downfall of the Rebellion.

"To make matters more complicated, we learned that your mother had become pregnant with you. She tried to persuade me to come here, to this realm, to have and to raise you far from P.O.R.T.A.L. and the Council's rule. But I must admit, I insisted we continue. For you see, I had stumbled upon a new hope.

"I was ... told of someone who I came to believe could finish my work and save the rebellion. After eight long months of searching for him, our quest brought us to your realm; the last free realm we ever discovered together.

"During our stay there, your mother grew increasingly worried that P.O.R.T.A.L. would find us. I also believed that my apprentice had become angry that I had chosen to turn my work over to someone else. I cannot fault him for that. But the truth is, I had grown wary of him. I suspected that he had become jealous of my relationship with your mother and my notoriety within the Rebellion.

"What happened next was tragic. One day, I returned to our hideout to find your mother's body on the floor; she'd been strangled. It seemed that my apprentice's jealousy and anger turned him against me, my wife, and the Rebellion. I rushed her to the nearest hospital, where I hoped they would be able to save our child. I wanted to go inside, but knew I'd be suspected of murder. I did the only thing I could and fled to this realm. I have been here in exile ever since."

"Wait, my mother didn't die in childbirth? She was murdered — by a traitor!" Atlas asked, enraged. "Who was your apprentice? I want to know who killed my mother?" Atlas's eyes blazed with fury.

Elio's face fell. He didn't answer right away. Finally, he said, "His name is Allister Craum, and he works for P.O.R.T.A.L."

Mia spun around at the sound of Craum's name, but she didn't move from her spot.

Atlas's face crumbled. "The man in the white suit ..."

Lilou shot Atlas a puzzled look. "Atlas, how do you know that?"

"When they took me to the hospital ward this morning, I overheard the soldiers talking about him. He's the one who interrogated us when we arrived at the prison."

Mia walked back to the sofa, her face red with anger. "Allister Craum is the man who arrested me and sentenced me to prison, he's also the man ..."

Elio interrupted. "Yes, my child, we all know the countless atrocities he has committed since the Fall. He has become an immensely powerful man with an abundance of resources at his disposal. And he's been hunting me ever since."

Mia sat back down on the sofa; her face contorted in anger.

"There's something I don't understand," Atlas said. "Why did you send us to Dr. Faraday that day? Is it because he's your ... twin?"

"Ahh, I see you have caught on; however, the correct term in the Multiverse is 'doppelganger.' You see, the Multiverse has endless possibilities. There are many realms almost identical to your own where you might find *your* doppelganger someday.

"But I sent you to him, because Malcolm Faraday was the *one* I was searching for. He is the one I believed could finish the work I started. He is also the reason I developed the voice transponder. After I exiled myself to this realm, I tried to find a way, from a safe distance, to pass on my knowledge to him. Discovering Faraday's frequency proved easy, as it was almost identical to mine.

"Once I established the connection, I secretly traveled to your realm and spoke to his unconscious mind while he was sleeping, feeding him the information he needed to develop his own transponder. He was almost there, but a tragedy befell him and his team of scientists, and he gave up his research. I hoped that sending you to him might reignite his interest in science so that he could one day fulfill his destiny."

"I thought you developed the voice transponder to find *me?*" Atlas asked.

Elio struggled to find his next words. "W-well, once I saw my success with Dr. Faraday, I realized that you might still be out there, and that your frequency might also be similar to mine. That's when I started looking for you," he explained, backtracking on his original story.

Atlas shook his head in disappointment. His father hadn't been honest about intending to find him.

Elio tried to divert the kids' attention. "Why don't we all get some rest, and tomorrow we can talk some more. You four can sleep upstairs in the loft, and I'll take the couch. How does that sound?"

Seeing how upset Atlas looked, Lilou stepped in to accept Elio's hospitality. "Thank you, that's very kind. We're all tired, so we'll head up now."

The four kids climbed the ladder to the loft. There they found one king-size bed and a large L-shaped sofa. "Atlas, why don't you and Nico take the bed, and Mia and I can take the couch," Lilou suggested.

"No, you two take the bed," was all Atlas said before throwing himself onto the sofa and retreating into his own thoughts.

He reflected on what he'd just heard. He had finally found his father, but every time Atlas learned some thing new it felt like they were taking two steps back. During his stay in prison, Atlas had believed his father developed the voice transponder to find him. Now he knew Elio had only developed it to continue his work with the Rebellion; searching for Atlas was an afterthought. What's more, knowing the horrible truth about his mother's death left him with many unanswered questions. Why would Allister Craum kill her? Was it really because he was jealous of his father? Atlas thought about his brief encounter with Craum in the prison interrogation room. Craum had been surprised to learn that Elio had a son; he obviously hadn't known that the unborn child had survived that night.

Atlas battled to keep his eyes open to remember more of their conversation that day, but exhaustion soon won, and he fell deeply asleep.

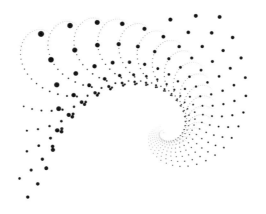

Chapter 12

Atlas woke up and found himself alone in the loft. He looked around and wondered where everyone was. He heard laughter coming from below. Peering over the loft's wooden railing, he saw Lilou, Nico, Mia, and Elio sitting around the small dining table, having breakfast. As Atlas descended the ladder, more laughter bubbled up from the table.

Elio looked up and said, "Atlas, my child, come, come, join us for breakfast. You can take a seat next to me." He was clearly in a good mood, probably, Atlas thought, because he hadn't had company in ages.

Atlas took the last open seat at the table.

Lilou smiled at him. "Your father is quite the storyteller," she said. "He was telling us about the time he ran into one of your mother's doppelgangers and saw her kissing another man. He thought she was cheating on him. He didn't believe her for an entire week. Isn't that something?"

"Don't worry Atlas. Your mother thought the whole thing was hilarious," Elio said. "She always had a wonderful sense of humor. In all the years we spent together, I never saw her go a day without at least one good belly laugh. I miss her laugh every day," he added, almost to himself.

"What was my mother's name?" Atlas asked.

"Elena — the most beautiful name for the most beautiful woman in all the Multiverse," Elio said with a smile. The conversation paused as Elio realized it might not be a good time to talk about Atlas's mother, whom he'd never known. "Atlas, you must be starving, you need to eat. When all of you are done, I'd like to show you my lab."

"You have a lab?" Nico asked, unable to hide his excitement.

"Oh, yes. It's built right into the mountain and took me many years to complete," Elio said with obvious pride. "I'll show you."

Atlas noticed that Mia had been sitting in gloomy silence. The wound on her right arm was now bandaged, likely courtesy of Elio. As breakfast ended, she left the table and walked out the front door. He soon followed and found her sitting on a small porch swing just big enough for the two of them.

"What are you doing out here? Aren't you cold?" Atlas asked, rubbing his hands together as he sat next to her.

"I thought I would hate him more. I do hate him. I just thought I would hate him more," Mia said glumly.

"You're talking about my father, aren't you?"

"Yes, your father."

"Yesterday, you said my father was the reason your father was dead. Can I ask what happened to him?" Atlas felt concerned for her, yet he worried that he was intruding.

"Your father believed what he was doing was best for everyone, but it was a lie."

"I don't understand. What was a lie?"

"His work. Your father is right. The Council wants to control the Multiverse, but they can only control what they know exists. There are billions of realms out there, and the only ones that pose a threat to their rule are those that have discovered interdimensional travel. Your father may have done what he thought was best, which was to share his technology and knowledge. But by doing that, he exposed new realms to the threat of P.O.R.T.A.L.

"If your father had never come to my realm, we would never have known that P.O.R.T.A.L. or the Council even existed — and we would still be free," Mia said, her voice full of resentment.

"Who was your father, anyway?"

"He was the greatest man I knew. He was a soldier. A general in the army. When our realm joined the Outliers Alliance, they put him in command of all forces. He fought and won many battles," she said with a proud smile. "But eventually, our realm fell, and with it, my father," she added sadly.

"Then you're not a rebel spy, are you?" Atlas asked, realizing this no longer made sense.

"No. I'm not a spy. After my father died, my mother and I fled to another realm. She was captured by P.O.R.T.A.L. and charged with treason, and I became nothing more than a street rat, until a band of smugglers took me in. I've been smuggling ever since. Until they caught me, of course."

A bit hurt, Atlas asked, "Then why did you lie to me, back in prison? I don't understand."

"I didn't mean to. I promise. It's just that the mole inside the prison thought I was a rebel. I believed he would only help me escape if I continued to pretend that I was a spy. Then I thought maybe you would only trust me if you thought I was a spy too. Remember, I'd been in that prison for over a year. I couldn't risk my only chance of escaping."

"So, you were never actually looking for my father?"

"Not exactly. A part of me wanted to find him so I could tell him to his face all the horrible things he'd done to my family. But after meeting him, it's clear he wouldn't care."

"I'm sorry about what happened to your father and your realm. I wish I knew how to help, but I'm still trying to learn who my father is and figure out my place in all this."

Atlas and Mia shared a moment of silence, before Atlas asked, "If you're not a spy, what about fighting those guards? Shooting those rifles? And flying that ship?"

"Most of it I learned from my father, and some I picked up as a smuggler," she said. She faced Atlas. "Atlas, you have to promise me that if you join the Rebellion, you won't make the same mistake your father did."

Atlas took a moment before he replied, "I promise," even though he wasn't entirely sure what joining the Rebellion meant. "Your mother, is she still out there?"

"I don't know. It's been four years since I've seen her. People charged with high treason aren't usually thrown into prison. They usually end up in Purgatory."

"Purgatory? Allister Craum — he said if he ever caught my father, he would send him to Purgatory. I also saw it on the building's map the day we escaped. What is Purgatory, exactly?"

"The worst thing imaginable. Think of a wormhole as a long hallway with two doors, one on each end. Now imagine if somebody shoved you into that hallway, then shut and locked the doors on both sides, never to be opened again." Mia shivered at the thought.

"Where do they go, what happens to them there?"

"Nobody really knows, because nobody has made it out to talk about it," Mia said glumly.

After a few moments, she said with forced cheerfulness, "Enough sad stories, we should get back. Your father is probably waiting."

They entered the cabin but found it empty.

"Is there a back door?" Atlas asked, looking around.

"I don't see one."

"Where could they have gone?"

"Look, somebody's moved the couch."

The couch was pushed to one side, exposing a hidden door in the floor and wooden steps leading down, below the cabin. Mia motioned for Atlas to go first. At the bottom, they found themselves in a massive underground cave.

Elio had clearly done a lot of work here. The floor was level and smooth. A large stone worktable sat in the center of the chamber. It was covered with strange instruments and tools, along with endless piles of paper. The walls held bulletin boards and big shelves on which sat more strange gadgets, maps, and diagrams. Some larger machines lined the walls. They appeared to be used for conducting experiments. On the wall to their left was an entire row of what looked like transponders of different shapes and sizes.

Elio, who was showing Nico a small handheld device, turned and greeted them. "Ah, good, you found us. I couldn't wait for you any longer, so we headed down here without you. I hope that was all right?" he asked. "I was just showing Nico my miniature particle accelerator. It uses focused magnetic fields to accelerate groups of particles."

"This is your lab?" Atlas said, looking around in amazement.

"Yes. I know it doesn't look like much, but it's the best I can do with the limited resources at my disposal.

I've conducted a lot of research and experiments down here. I even built the voice transponder that I used to contact you here in this lab," Elio said. He seemed happy to have an opportunity to remind Atlas that he'd used the voice transponder to find him.

"Are those transponders too?" Atlas said, pointing to the devices hanging on the wall.

"Ah, yes. As you can see, they come in various shapes and sizes, depending on which realm they're from. Many are my own design."

Atlas paced while Mia explored the unusual-looking machines and devices. "Maybe you already answered this, but where are we exactly?" Atlas said, realizing he didn't know which realm they were in.

"This is another uncharted realm, not on any map, and far from the outstretched arms of P.O.R.T.A.L.," Elio replied, skirting around an actual answer.

Nico put in, "You said yesterday that our realm was one of the last free realms you found, but what about this realm, is it free of the Council's rule?"

"Yes. This realm is also free, but it is a primitive realm with no humans, and therefore of little value to the Council. As you now know, the Multiverse is full of endless possibilities. Therefore, there are millions of realms almost identical to your own, which we classify as Class B realms. The realm you three are originally from, I call Earth B33. There are also realms that are more technologically advanced than yours, like Earth A14, the realm in which they imprisoned you. And then there are Class C realms, which are developing realms that possess only primitive technology — like this one," Elio explained.

"If there are no people here, and no power grid, what powers your machines?" Atlas asked, looking around for a power source.

Nico answered for Elio. "He must use thermal energy from the mountain. This lab must sit on top of a small volcano."

Elio beamed at Nico. "Brilliant observation, Nico. I am impressed. Through those passageways over there, I have a machine that converts the mountain's thermal energy into electricity. It's virtually an endless power source for my research."

"What's this?" Lilou said, pointing to a device sitting on a small display.

"Please, don't touch that!" Elio rushed over and carefully picked up the instrument, almost cradling it in his hands. "This is my new transponder. This is what is going to restore the Rebellion."

"Really? How does it work?" Nico asked.

"When I developed my voice transponder, I discovered that all living things emit their own frequency. So if you know someone's life-frequency, you can travel straight to them."

Atlas looked at Elio. "Yesterday, when we were escaping, you said you've made progress. What did you mean?"

"I've modified this new device to detect the subtle frequencies emitted from all living things. If you can detect the frequencies of the living things around you, you can open a wormhole virtually anywhere," his father replied.

"I don't understand," Atlas said. "How does detecting the frequencies from living things help you do this?"

Once again, Nico answered for Elio. "It uses triangulation. Like how seismologists detect the location of an earthquake's epicenter."

"Excellent, Nico. Right again. Your intuition is breathtaking," Elio said, placing a hand on Nico's shoulder. "When I opened the wormhole to your bedroom that day, I proved that the technology works. I entered Atlas's frequency into my transponder, and it worked like any other coordinate, opening a portal directly in front of you.

"And that's not all. When I'm finished, the transponder will use triangulation, as Nico explained, to create a three-dimensional map of the world around you. You can then travel to precise locations, even over very short distances," he concluded.

Atlas glanced at Nico with a hint of jealousy, then back at his father. "Why would you need to travel over short distances?"

"Imagine being on a battlefield where you could open a portal in front of you and another one behind your enemy, allowing you to flank the enemy and take them by surprise. You could also bypass any locked door or free prisoners from their cells. No current transponder is accurate enough to do that.

"For the transponder to be that precise, it must create new wormholes — ones that don't already exist. The problem is, right now, those new wormholes are too unstable, and I'm afraid they may collapse if someone tries to pass through them."

"How do we stabilize them?" Nico asked.

"More energy. Transponders use quantum reactions to generate the power needed to open wormholes, but traditional radioactive elements have proven insufficient for my new transponder," Elio said despondently.

Mia, who had been silent until now, said, "Then you need something like Element X."

Elio chuckled. "There's no such thing as Element X," he smirked, clearly thinking the idea was ridiculous.

Mia scowled at him. "Yes, there is. And P.O.R.T.A.L. has already started mining for it."

"Mining for it, where?" Elio asked. He sounded interested despite his skepticism.

"Earth C19," Atlas mumbled, remembering the story Mia had told him about Esme's home realm. "Earth C19. They are mining for it there," he said loudly.

"Are you sure? How can you know that?" Elio said.

"I'm sure. It's there."

"Allister Craum ... What's he up to?" Elio murmured. He took a seat, looking agitated.

"I'm sorry, but what's Element X?" Lilou asked.

"It's believed to be dark matter in its solid-state," Elio replied. "It's theorized that Element X is formed when a dying universe collapses in on itself. Element X is theorized to emit or radiate an endless supply of dark energy."

"If we can get you Element X, can you finish your transponder?" Lilou asked.

"Yes, of course. Even the smallest amount would be more than enough to power my new transponder. But where are we going to get it?"

"We're gonna go to Earth C19 to steal it," Lilou declared.

"We're gonna do *what?*" Atlas cried. Not waiting for an answer, Atlas asked Elio, "Do you mind if I have a minute with my brother and sister alone?" He grabbed Lilou and Nico by their arms and pulled them aside. "Lilou, what are you talking about? I thought you wanted to go home?" he whispered loudly.

"I did, and we will. But first we need to take care of business here. After I heard what Allister Craum did to your mother, I realized he's nothing more than a big bully, and you know that I do not like bullies. Atlas, do you remember how good it felt to throw your lunch tray at that bully Zack back in the school cafeteria?" Lilou said with a smile, reminding Atlas of his small victory.

Atlas smiled back and nodded. Ever since he'd heard about his mother's death, he'd felt conflicted about what to do next. Lilou's support was the confidence boost he needed. "Nico, what about you, are you okay with this?" Atlas asked.

"Are you asking if I want to be one of the first people in the Multiverse to lay my hands on a rare element and use it to power a device that will allow you to travel anywhere?" Nico said, deadpan.

Atlas and Lilou looked at each other, puzzled by his lack of enthusiasm.

Nico's face broke into a wide smile. "Yes, the answer is yes, if that wasn't clear."

"Okay, then we do this together," Atlas said.

"As a family," Lilou added with a grin.

The siblings walked back to Elio. "Atlas, you don't need to do this for me. It's too dangerous ..." Elio started to say.

"We're not doing this for you," Atlas said. He looked at Mia, thinking about what he now knew about her parents and her home realm. "We're doing it for the people who never had a choice, and those still locked up in P.O.R.T.A.L. prisons across the Multiverse," he continued. "When your transponder is finished, we're going back to free all the prisoners we left behind. Now, how do we get to Earth C19?"

Elio threw up his hands in surrender and grabbed three transponders off the wall. "Here, each of you needs to take one of these. They're pre-programmed with every known realm in the System, including some unknown to P.O.R.T.A.L. You won't need to type in any coordinates, just the destination," he said.

"We'll need four of them," Mia said drily.

"Mia, you don't have to come with us. We can help you get home now," Atlas whispered, wanting to tell her in private.

"Home? And where is that, exactly?" she said. "Besides, how did you plan on stealing Element X from under P.O.R.T.A.L.'s nose, anyway? I'm a smuggler, remember? You need me."

Atlas smiled and nodded in acceptance. He knew he wasn't going to convince Mia otherwise, and that they did need her help to pull this off. He turned his attention back to Elio. "Okay, how do we get back here when we're done?"

"First, you must remember to realm-hop. Don't come straight back, or P.O.R.T.A.L. might be able to follow you. After you realm-hop, you'll find that this realm has been programmed into your transponders under the keycode Elena, after your dear mother. Enter that into your transponder, and it will bring you back to this mountainside."

"What do you mean by realm-hop?" Lilou asked.

Mia said, "He means we need to travel to an uncharted realm first before traveling to and from Earth C19, just like we did before coming here. It's how he must have avoided being tracked all these years. It's an old smuggler's trick."

"Okay, then what uncharted realm are we supposed to use?" Lilou asked, looking at Elio anxiously.

"Hmm, let me see ... I try not to use the same realm too often," Elio replied, studying one of his many maps hanging on the cave walls. "Ah, here we are. You can use Uncharted 5. I haven't used it in years. But be careful; it's a prehistoric realm. The last time I was there, I found myself in the middle of a herd of angry triceratops."

"Wait — are you talking about dinosaurs?" Lilou said in disbelief.

"Correct. It's classified as a Class D realm, because humans never evolved there. In this particular realm, the asteroid that you know killed the dinosaurs sixty-six million years ago never hit the earth; therefore, dinosaurs never went extinct," Elio explained. "Now, here. You'll also need these," he added, opening a drawer and pulling out four voice transponders.

"How do we use them?" Lilou said, examining the small devices.

"Turn them on, put the transponder in your ear, and pair them with each other's minds. To do that, hold down the small red button on the back of the device and say each of your names out loud. Once they're paired, simply hold down the button and say the name of the person you want to speak to. The voice transponder will do the rest.

"I gave each of you your own voice transponder. But like a traditional transponder, only one device is required at a time to establish a connection. And remember, these devices cannot be used to communicate across realms, so once you leave this realm, I can no longer help you," he said, emphasizing the dangerous nature of their mission.

"Mia," Atlas said, "after we realm-hop, how do we travel to Earth C19 without P.O.R.T.A.L. tracking us once we arrive?"

"Earth C19 is a mining realm, which means P.O.R.T.A.L. is constantly transporting supplies in and out of it. If we open a wormhole outside the city, it will be sure to draw attention, and we'll be captured. Our only chance is to open a wormhole inside the city limits and hope it doesn't raise a red flag. Plus, we'll need to close the wormhole as soon as we're through and get as far away from that location as possible."

"Here, take this one," Elio said, removing a sleek, diamond-shaped, black transponder from the wall and handing it to Mia. "I stole this from P.O.R.T.A.L. years ago. I've never used it, because I feared they could use it to track me. But it's been twelve years, and it's the only one precise enough to get you inside the city limits."

"And what city are we going to, exactly?" Lilou asked.

"Giza," Mia replied.

"Egypt — of course. Our tan jumpsuits will fit right in," Lilou said with a chuckle.

"Well, what are we waiting for? Atlas, open the wormhole," Mia directed.

Atlas nodded. He turned on his transponder, searched for Uncharted 5, and opened a portal inside the lab.

All four put their voice transponders in their ears and paired them before stepping forward to stand in front of the portal.

Just before they went in, Nico turned to Elio. "What does Element X look like?" he asked.

"Nico, I'm confident that you will know it when you see it," Elio replied. "Now, good luck to you all."

Atlas faced Lilou and Nico. "The last time I opened a wormhole, I didn't give either of you a choice, and I'm sorry about that. This time, I still want to be holding your hands, but I want to walk through together."

With the transponders safely around their necks, Lilou grabbed Nico's hand and Atlas's. They all turned to Mia, who took Atlas's other hand, and the four of them entered the wormhole and vanished.

***

"Where are the children off to now?" a sinister voice spoke from behind Elio. "Oh, never mind. It doesn't matter. We have them attached to a string. We'll pick them up soon enough."

Elio turned to see Allister Craum slowly walking down the stairs into his lab, followed by armed soldiers in white tactical gear.

"Allister, it's been a long time. I see you're still doing the Council's bidding," Elio said, backing away from them.

"If you knew the truth about the Council, you would be too. But that has always been your problem, hasn't it, Elio? Everything is black and white, good vs. evil. P.O.R.T.A.L. vs. the Outliers Alliance. What is the difference? Both are fighting for the same thing: control of the Multiverse. There is no good and evil — only winners and losers. And guess which one you are right now?" Craum said.

Two of his soldiers walked around the sides of the table, cutting off Elio's escape routes. One grabbed Elio and forced his hands behind his back; the other gave him a hard punch to the gut.

Elio, bent over in pain and struggling for air, asked, "Elena. Why did you kill her?"

Allister Craum scoffed. "We all know Elena was brilliant, but that child made her wise. She knew the truth about the Council. She foresaw that the Rebellion would end in failure and convinced me that the time to switch sides was upon us. We began making plans to defect. Secret plans, of course, since Elena wanted everything laid out perfectly before bringing you in. We started collecting data and information that we hoped would grant us immunity and admittance into P.O.R.T.A.L. Everything would have worked flawlessly, except that her pitiful love for you blinded her into believing that you could be converted too.

"I knew, however, that you would never turn against the Rebellion, and I couldn't risk you finding out, not after everything I'd worked so hard to steal. So I did what I had to do," Craum said coolly.

"Liar! That's not true, Elena would never!" Elio shouted, struggling against the hands that held him.

The soldier gave him another punch to the gut, this time bringing Elio to his knees.

"Get bindings on him and throw him on the transport. I don't want to see his face anymore," Craum said impassively.

The soldiers bound Elio's hands and wrists and carried him up the stairs. As Elio passed Craum, he said, "Where are you taking me?"

"Fool. Why do you ask questions to which you already know the answer?"

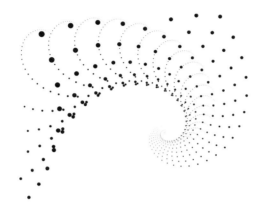

Chapter 13

A tlas, Lilou, Nico, and Mia emerged into the middle of the barren desert. Looking around, Lilou said, "Good. I don't see any dinosaurs."

Nico looked disappointed. "I wouldn't have minded seeing a few," he said.

Atlas closed the portal behind them and turned to Mia. "Mia. Do it."

She took out the stolen transponder and entered Earth C19-Giza into its interface, opening another portal.

They stepped through and found themselves inside a large stone building. Lining its interior walls were giant stone columns and stone statues of god-like figures with various animal heads. The largest statue was of a woman with the head of an eagle. Her arms were held outstretched in front of her with her palms facing up. Water flowed out of her chest, down her arms, and spilled over her fingertips like a waterfall, into a giant pool at the center of room. Vines along the walls and large exotic plants created an almost jungle-like atmosphere. Several men and women were lazily floating in the large pool, talking among themselves. When they saw the four kids, they began shouting in a foreign language. The minute Mia closed the portal behind them, the young intruders slowly backpedaled. Mia spotted a staircase and shouted, "Up those stairs! Let's go!"

As they ran up the giant stone staircase, Atlas asked, almost out of breath, "What is this place?"

"I believe we're in a bathhouse. They were quite popular in the Middle East and Africa," Nico replied.

At the top of the stairs, Lilou noticed two rows of clothing hanging from hooks on a wall. "Quick, let's put these on. They'll help us blend in," she said.

They replaced their tan jumpsuits with robes and headgear that must have belonged to the men and women below. When they were dressed, they couldn't help but stare at each other. Lilou said, "This reminds me of the time we had to dress up in history class for that simulation of Ancient Egypt."

"Yeah, except those robes didn't smell so bad," Atlas replied. He flared his nostrils at the foul stench coming from his robe.

Mia said, "Come on. We need to keep moving. If P.O.R.T.A.L. detected our wormhole, they're probably already on their way."

The four found the bathhouse's exit. Outside, they were greeted by blinding sun and scorching heat. Atlas, temporarily unable to see, bumped into someone's back. As his eyes adjusted to the light, he realized he'd walked into a P.O.R.T.A.L. soldier standing guard outside.

The soldier turned to see who had dared to bump into him. "What are you staring at, kid?" he said. "Get out of my face before I lock you up for the night."

Atlas, shocked that his face hadn't given him away, bowed his head and walked away briskly. The others followed close behind.

Once they'd put distance between themselves and the soldier, Mia whispered, "We need to be more careful. That could have been the end of our mission."

Lilou, now in the lead, turned the corner at the end of the narrow alleyway and stopped dead. "Umm guys ... are you seeing this?"

"Is that what I think it is?" Atlas asked.

"Yeah — that's definitely a pyramid," Mia said. "And look, there are dozens of them in all directions."

"This civilization appears to have many parallels to our ancient Egypt," Nico put in.

"That one's gigantic ..." Lilou trailed off in wonder, staring at the pyramid at the end of the street nearest to them.

The pyramids didn't look like the old, weather-beaten ones they'd seen in their history books at school. The exteriors were flat and made of polished white stone. No lines or imperfections could be seen from their position. Atop each pyramid was a shiny gold capstone that reflected the sun's rays.

"Let's keep moving. We need to get as far away from that bathhouse as possible," Mia urged them.

Exiting the alleyway, they found themselves in the middle of an expansive bazaar. Hundreds of street vendors were selling every kind of goods and services. A loud, insistent chatter could be heard as merchants and customers conversed, shouted, and haggled. Sinuous music played in the distance.

Atlas scanned the busy street and saw several P.O.R.T.A.L. soldiers on patrol. Two of them appeared to be on a two-seater hovercraft. It wove in and out of the crowds of people. "There are soldiers everywhere," he said.

"We need to keep a low profile. Make sure your transponders aren't visible," Mia said, pulling her robe tighter to cover the device around her neck.

As they headed toward one of the massive pyramids, Atlas saw a pair of soldiers jogging toward them.

Mia quickly turned and pretended to check out the fruits and vegetables at a vendor stand. The siblings followed suit as the soldiers passed behind them, turned the corner, and headed down an alleyway.

"Where do you think they're going?" Atlas whispered.

Mia said anxiously, "To the bathhouse. They must have tracked our wormhole. They know someone is here."

"Then we need to hurry. We need to find Element X and get out of here," Atlas said.

"But we don't know where to look," Lilou said.

Mia pointed at the sky. "See all those cargo ships? They're all headed to or from the pyramids."

Cargo ships were indeed exiting giant portals in the sky and flying toward the pyramids, while other ships were leaving the pyramids near their capstones and flying toward the portals.

"The mines must be below the pyramids," Nico surmised.

Trusting Nico's intuition, Atlas said, "Then that's where we need to go. That's where we'll find Element X."

"But which one do we go to?" Lilou asked.

"That big one," Atlas said, pointing down the street.

The two soldiers that had run past them returned to the bazaar. Atlas overheard him question a third soldier, the one he'd bumped into when he left the bathhouse. "What did they look like?"

"There were four in total, but I only got a good look at the one. He was tall, but young. I suspect we're looking for four teenagers."

"Roger that, I'm calling it in. You two, use your Geiger counters to track them," the soldier said. He stepped aside to use his radio.

As soon as the kids saw him pull out this radio, they hustled in the opposite direction, turned down the next alleyway, and started to run.

"Wait, they can track us?" Lilou said breathlessly.

Mia replied, "To some degree. When you pass through a wormhole, your body picks up a lot of radiation, which can be detected using a Geiger counter. As long as we keep moving, the radiation should wear off soon. Quick, in here." She pushed through a wooden door into a small, abandoned building. "Those soldiers know they're looking for four teenagers. We'll have to split up. We'll be too obvious traveling together."

"We should take two different streets and meet at the pyramid," Atlas said.

"No, that will draw too much attention," Nico responded.

"Why?"

"All our tracks will lead in the same direction, and the soldiers will converge on the pyramid. We need to draw some of the soldiers away from it," Nico added.

"I have an idea," Lilou said.

They all looked at her in surprise.

"Atlas, go to that pyramid and find Element X. Take Mia with you, because you'll need her help to smuggle it out. Nico and I will walk away from the pyramid. When you give the signal, we'll create a diversion and lead as many soldiers away from that pyramid as we can."

"What kind of diversion?" Atlas asked, both intrigued and concerned.

"Don't worry about that now, just trust me," Lilou said.

"Lilou, this sounds dangerous."

"Atlas, it's the only way. Listen, we all knew what we were getting into."

"Okay, fine, let's do this." Atlas realized they needed to get moving.

He and Mia left the building first. They continued down the alleyway and turned right at the next major street, which led straight to the giant pyramid. Every major street appeared to converge there. The road they were on was adjacent to the bazaar, but much less busy. It appeared to be a residential street. Women were hanging clothes on clotheslines, families were laughing, and children were playing tag in the middle of the street. Atlas saw no soldiers. He hoped this meant that the street was less patrolled than the bazaar. As they got further down the street, Atlas heard Lilou's voice in his head.

Atlas, can you hear me?

"Yes, I can. Can you hear me?" Atlas replied out loud so Mia could listen in to their conversation.

Whoa, this is so weird. It's like you're inside my head.

"Yeah, I know. Strange, right?" Atlas replied, recalling his attempts to explain it to his siblings back home. "Where are you guys?"

We took a few turns and found our way back to the market. There are soldiers everywhere now, waving these wands. It looks like they're trying to pick up on our radiation tracks but having difficulty. Nico thinks changing our clothes might have helped. We're going to stay in the market and move away from the pyramid to draw them off. Let me know when you get close to the pyramid.

"Okay. Be safe, and if you think you're going to be captured, open a wormhole, and get out of here. Mia and I will finish the job."

Atlas and Mia continued toward the pyramid, keeping their heads down and trying to look inconspicuous. Soon, the pyramid appeared to grow even larger, until it engulfed the sky.

"Look, up there," Mia said. "The cargo ships are leaving through the hole in the top of the pyramid. They must extract the element below ground, then send it directly up the pyramid and onto the ships."

"But what are they putting on all those ships if this element is so rare?"

"Hmm, they must not be removing it here. Perhaps they're taking large chunks of earth and moving them somewhere first. If that's the case, this might be more difficult to steal than I thought."

"Let's worry about that after we get inside," Atlas said.

Atlas, I hope you guys are getting close, because we've hit a dead end. Nico and I may have stumbled on the soldiers' barracks. It looks like the city is lined with them.

"Okay, keep your heads down. We're gonna try to find a way inside now."

"Was that your sister? What did she say?" Mia asked.

"Nothing. We just need to keep moving," Atlas said, not wanting to alarm her.

"Look, at the bottom. See those people entering and leaving the pyramid? They look like they're enslaved. P.O.R.T.A.L. must use them to mine for Element X."

Enslaved people, Atlas thought, remembering Mia's story about what had happened here on Earth C19. "We need to get in that line. That's our way in," he said.

Atlas! Nico and I will be right back! I hope you are close because your diversion will be here soon.

"Lilou, what diversion? Lilou, are you still there?" Atlas said aloud, but he heard nothing more.

"Where did they go?" Mia said.

"I have no idea. She's not answering. But she said our diversion is coming soon."

They shared a look of concern, before moving closer to the pyramid. They eventually found a large crowd entering the building. They were grabbing pickaxes from large crates on the ground. Although initially worried that he and Mia might stand out, Atlas was relieved to see that the people were of all ages and skin tones, and they wore various types of clothing. Once in line, Atlas and Mia took two pickaxes from the crates and followed the people in front of them. As they continued walking, Atlas saw soldiers everywhere. They were patrolling the lines, using batons to motivate the people to move faster, patrolling the perimeter of the pyramid, and standing guard by the entryway.

Up ahead, Atlas saw a soldier checking the prisoners for radiation with a Geiger counter wand.

"Mia, he's going to find us," Atlas whispered.

"We need to draw the soldiers away. Tell your brother and sister we need that diversion now," Mia whispered back.

Atlas reached up to his ear, partially covered by his large hood, and pushed the voice transponder. "Lilou, are you there?"

Yes, we're back, and we brought some friends with us.

"Back from where? What friends?"

Just then, he heard a soldier patrolling the line respond to a radio call. "What do you mean, there are dinosaurs in the barracks?"

"Yes, you heard me, dinosaurs! An entire herd of them. Send backup now!" a voice over the radio cried.

Dinosaurs ... Atlas thought.

"Did that soldier say dinosaurs?" Mia asked.

"Lilou and Nico must have gone back to the uncharted realm and brought them back," Atlas said.

All around them, soldiers abandoned their posts and jumped on hovercrafts. Atlas turned his attention to the soldier with the wand. He held his breath as the soldier passed the wand to one of his comrades and shouted, "Here, take this with you. They're out there somewhere. This will help you find them."

Now only a handful of soldiers remained to watch the pyramid.

It worked! Atlas thought.

As they approached the entryway, Atlas's nerves returned. His heart raced as he sized up the remaining two soldiers standing guard. If he and Mia were captured, their fate would be far worse than being thrown back into prison. He glanced back at her, almost hoping she would tell him they should abort the mission. But turning back toward the guards, he saw that they were distracted by the chaos they were hearing over their radios.

He and Mia walked right past them and into the pyramid.

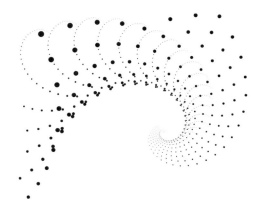

Chapter 14

Inside the pyramid, Atlas was surprised to find ample evidence of P.O.R.T.A.L.'s advanced technology. The interior had been transformed into a P.O.R.T.A.L. outpost. Along the walls were large panel lights and rows of wires. There were also ceiling cameras and video monitors that displayed instructions to the enslaved workers.

Shortly after walking in, they were sprayed down with a mist released through tiny holes in the ceiling. "What's this?" Atlas whispered to Mia.

"Maybe it's a decontamination protocol. We'll probably go through the same thing on our way out."

If we make it out, he thought. "Look," he said softly. "The workers are piling into that big room up ahead."

As they got closer to the room, two soldiers standing guard stopped the line short of the entrance. One of them pushed a button on his computer. Atlas and Mia watched as the room — actually a giant elevator — was lowered into the ground.

When the elevator returned a minute later, the soldiers ushered on more prisoners. As Atlas and Mia passed the soldiers, Atlas pulled his robe tight to hide his transponder. When the space was filled to capacity, they too were lowered into the mines. They were surprised that the elevator traveled at high speed, plummeting deep into the earth. After what felt like only seconds, the elevator gently came to a stop.

A maze of mineshafts led out from the elevator in every direction. The air in the mine was dense, sticky, and dusty, making it hard to breathe. Above the tunnels' entryways, signs were posted in an unfamiliar language.

"Where do we go from here?" Atlas said.

"Don't ask me. Let's just pick one."

As they walked through one of the poorly lit tunnels, they passed a group of workers chipping away at the earth and loading big chunks of rock onto carts to be transported elsewhere. At one point, Atlas bent down to examine one of the chunks of rock to look for anything out of the ordinary.

"I don't understand. It just looks like a regular rock," he said to Mia.

"Let's just keep looking," she said.

"Wait, you're the one that knew about it. What is it supposed to look like?"

"Don't ask me. I've never seen it before. I've only heard stories."

I wish Nico was here, Atlas thought.

As Atlas stood, Lilou's voice inside his head shouted, *Atlas! Can you hear me? You need to get out of there! He's here. It's a tra ...*

"Lilou! Lilou! Where are you? Who's here?" Atlas shouted back in his mind, but there was no response. He turned to Mia and said, "Mia, it's Lilou, they're in trou ..." before he heard another voice inside his head, one he didn't recognize right away.

Atlas, is that you, dear boy?

"Who is this and what have you done with my brother and sister?" Atlas said out loud.

Oh, I'm just an old friend of your mother and father. I see your father finally finished his voice transponder he spent so many years blabbing on about.

Allister Craum ... Atlas thought, forgetting that Craum could hear his thoughts.

Very good. Now, why don't you come up from that mine and we can sort this whole thing out.

"Why? So you can send us back to that prison of yours? I don't think so," using his internal voice.

Ah yes, your daring escape. How heroic of you. I will admit, I did not plan on you taking so many prisoners with you in the process, and for that, I shall never forgive myself.

"What do you mean, you didn't plan on me taking prisoners?"

You silly boy. Did you actually think you escaped on your own? You're as pathetic as your father. I let you escape. I told you that you were going to help me find your father, remember? It was really quite simple, thanks to the help of your little friend.

Atlas turned and looked Mia in the eyes, worried yet skeptical about what Craum was implying about her.

"Atlas, what is it?" she said. "Who are you speaking to?"

Atlas said to Craum, "What are you going to do with my brother and sister?"

The same thing I will do to you if you don't come out of that mine right now!

"I'm not coming up there!"

I'm starting to lose my temper, boy. I'm giving you one last chance to turn yourself in, or I'm coming down there to personally see that you spend the rest of your existence in Purgatory. Do you understand me?

Atlas wanted to shout back. He wanted to know if Mia had helped Craum, and to grill Craum about his mother. But he knew this would only waste the little time he had. He calmed his mind and pushed Craum out, ending their communication. Atlas turned to Mia. "They're coming," he said.

"Who's coming? Where are Lilou and Nico?"

"Allister Craum is here, and he's captured them. The next elevator will likely be filled with soldiers."

"Captured? Atlas, I can't go back to prison," Mia replied, agitated. "We still have the transponder, we can open a wormhole and leave now," she reminded him, taking out the transponder around her neck.

"No, I need to finish the mission. I need to find Element X and get back to my father. He could be in danger, and it's the only way to rescue Lilou and Nico." He threw the pickaxe over his shoulder and walked further into the mine. "Are you coming?" he said, closely watching Mia's reaction.

She nodded and followed him. As they walked, they continued analyzing the walls and piles of rock, looking for anything out of the ordinary. They began to feel that they'd exhausted all hope.

"I don't understand. I don't see anything," Atlas said. "Maybe it's not here? I mean, this mine could be for anything."

"I guess you're right." Atlas remembered it was he who thought Element X might be there. "It's not here. We came here for nothing, and now Lilou and Nico have been captured," he said, falling to his knees.

"Shhh ..." Mia sounded. "Do you hear that?"

"Hear what? I don't hear anything."

"Exactly ... the workers have stopped mining. Craum must be here."

Atlas spotted the shadow of a soldier creeping around the bend of the tunnel behind Mia. "Mia, run!" he shouted. He jumped to his feet and they both ran from the soldier. Behind them, soldiers shouted orders as they closed in.

"We need to get far enough away so that we can open a wormhole!" Atlas yelled. He slowed down to pull his transponder off his neck and get it ready. When he looked back up, he saw Mia at a dead stop staring downward. He looked over his shoulder. A soldier was coming around the corner, raising his rifle to his shoulder. A flurry of energy pulses darted past him, hitting the surrounding walls and spraying dirt all over him.

He ran toward Mia. "Mia, move!" he yelled, and instinctively tackled her. They tumbled down a steep hill, deeper into the earth. After falling head over feet for what felt like minutes, they landed on a flat surface. Before they could check themselves for injuries, a coughing fit overtook them due to the thick dust and dirt that covered them from head to toe.

When they regained the energy to stand, they realized they were at the bottom of a giant cave. The air was even more oppressive and muggy than in the mineshafts above. Atlas looked at the cave opening. A soldier in a white tactical uniform stood there, clearly awaiting orders.

"Mia, we need to open the wormhole!" Atlas shouted, tossing her the transponder clenched in his hand.

She caught it, turned it on, typed Uncharted 5 into the interface, and hit enter. Atlas took a last look at the soldier at the top and entered the portal behind Mia.

Once safely through, they checked their surroundings, which were happily devoid of animal life, and closed the portal. Mia entered Elena into the transponder to open the wormhole that would take them back to the cabin.

Stepping through it, they found themselves on the mountainside. The portal had opened behind Elio's cabin, but farther up the mountain. After closing the portal, Atlas and Mia sprinted full speed toward the cabin.

Rushing inside, Atlas shouted, "Elio! Elio! Lilou and Nico have been captured!" Not seeing Elio anywhere, he ran to the trapdoor and down the stairs into the lab. At the bottom was a very different scene from the one they'd left. Papers were strewn across the floor, and most of Elio's lab equipment had been destroyed or taken. Atlas searched the nearby rooms, shouting, "Elio! Where are you?" But he was nowhere to be found.

"He's gone, they've taken him," Atlas said.

"I don't understand. How did they find him?"

Atlas paused, remembering what Allister Craum had said about Mia. "You ... you did this, you led them here," Atlas said, glaring at Mia.

She scowled. "What are you talking about? I had nothing to do with this," she said.

"Back in the pyramid, Allister Craum said he allowed us to escape and that you helped him do it."

"Atlas, you have to believe me. I didn't do this. We planned that escape together, remember? You and me."

"No, you planned the escape, and you lied to me and said you were a spy."

"Atlas, I've explained this to you. I wanted you to trust me, and I thought the mole would only help us if he thought we were rebels."

"Wait ... say that again."

"I said, I wanted you to trust me."

"No, about the mole," Atlas said sharply.

"That he would only help if he thought we were rebels?" Mia said, confused.

"The mole ... Mia, how long did you know that mole?"

"I don't know. He started communicating with me around the same time we met. Why?"

"How could you have not told me that before? The mole was obviously working for Craum. Craum planned the whole thing, and we fell into his trap."

"But why? I don't understand, why would he want us to escape?"

"Because he wanted us to lead him to my father."

"But we didn't lead him to your father. We escaped, and we realm-hopped just like we were supposed to. So how could they have found this place?"

Atlas realized that Mia was right. Even if Craum had planned their escape, it didn't explain how he had tracked them down.

"He would have needed a tracking device to lead them here," Mia guessed.

Atlas thought back to his encounter with the doctor in the hospital ward. He put his right hand on his left shoulder. "The shots. One of the shots must have been to implant a tracking device into my arm. Mia, we have to get it out! They've been tracking me, that's what led them here. And that's what led them to Earth C19 to capture Lilou and Nico."

"You have a tracking device in your arm?" Mia asked, dismayed.

"Yes. And now it will lead them back here. We need to get it out, now!" he said, scratching at his arm.

Mia grabbed his arm. "Atlas, stop. Let me look at it. I think I can see it. But it's too small. There's no way we'll get it out. But maybe we can disable it."

"Disable it? How?"

"We'll need a magnet, a strong one."

Atlas scanned the lab for anything that looked like a magnet. Then he remembered. "The miniature particle accelerator. Elio said it uses electromagnets. Quick, see if it is still here."

Atlas and Mia frantically searched the lab, hoping the accelerator hadn't been destroyed. After a few moments Atlas shouted, "I found it! It was underneath a pile of papers under the table." He held up the intact donut-shaped instrument.

"Good," Mia said. "Put your arm through the hole in the accelerator, and I'll turn it on. The electromagnetic field should be strong enough to disable the tracker."

Atlas carefully placed his arm through the hole. When Mia flipped the on switch, the accelerator buzzed, indicating it was working. After a few minutes, she flipped the switch off, and Atlas pulled his arm out.

"There, it's done. But how do we know it worked?" she asked.

"We don't," Atlas replied.

"Then what do we do now?"

Atlas turned and faced away from Mia. "Mia, you need to go. It's not safe here. If they can still track me, they'll be here soon. They've already captured my family. I can't let them capture you, too."

"Atlas, I'm not leaving you."

"Yes, you are," Atlas said. He turned and faced Mia again, holding his transponder. Mia saw that Earth A27 had been entered into the keypad. She turned around to find an open portal. Before she could speak, Atlas pulled her transponder off her neck and pushed her into the light.

***

"They're gone, sir. They fell into a pit down in the mines and opened a wormhole before we had a chance to follow," a soldier said as he walked out of the giant pyramid covered in dust, followed by the rest of Allister Craum's personal guards.

"I don't want to hear about your failures. Tell me how long it will take to find them!" Craum demanded, trying to contain his rage.

"You'll never find my brother, you pointy-nosed pathetic excuse for a man!" Lilou screamed from off in the distance behind Craum.

"What did you just say to me, little girl?" Craum said, scowling at Lilou.

"I said, you have a pointy nose," Lilou replied defiantly.

"Why hasn't anyone put a muzzle on this annoying juvenile yet!" He faced the soldier from the mine again. "I want them out of my sight, now!" Craum cried.

"Yes sir." The soldier started to march Lilou and Nico onto a nearby transport.

"Wait ... bring them back," Craum said more calmly.

The soldier hesitated, looking confused, then hustled Lilou and Nico back to Craum.

"I know why you and your little friends were here. Now tell me, what did Elio plan on doing with the element anyway?"

"He is building a weapon more powerful than anything you've ever seen. One capable of destroying entire realms," Lilou declared.

"A weapon?" Nico whispered.

Lilou gave Nico a subtle bump with her elbow to indicate he should keep his mouth shut.

Craum smirked. "You fools. Elio won't be building anything in Purgatory. You know, I'm almost disappointed that he won't have the chance to see what I'm developing for his little Alliance." He motioned for the soldier to take Lilou and Nico away again.

"Sir, we just had a lock on his signal, but it disappeared," the soldier said.

"Where was the signal transmitting from?" Craum replied, visibly upset.

"Elio's hideout, Sir. Do you want us to send a squadron?"

Craum turned and watched Lilou and Nico enter the transport. "No. We have what we need. He will come to us, and when he does, I'll be waiting."

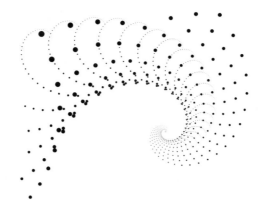

Chapter 15

S ince there was no guarantee that the tracking device had been disabled, Atlas knew his only choice was to send Mia away. He had already lost his sister, brother, and father. He couldn't risk losing his only real friend as well. He took comfort in knowing that the Outliers Alliance controlled Earth A27, and it would serve as a safe refuge for her. He also knew that the only way to verify that the tracking device was no longer transmitting a signal to P.O.R.T.A.L. was to wait and find out. So that's what he resolved to do.

Atlas spent the next hour in the lab searching to see if P.O.R.T.A.L. had left any of Elio's machines or inventions intact. He saw that they had taken all the transponders from the wall. He had his and Mia's transponders, and he still had his voice transponder in his ear.

Atlas remembered his father's new transponder and anxiously wondered if they'd taken that too. He looked at the display case where Lilou had discovered it. Unsurprisingly, it was empty. His father had been showing it to them. Might it have fallen to the floor during the commotion?

Atlas dropped to his hands and knees and dug through the papers and pieces of broken machines scattered about the floor, hoping that, like the particle accelerator, it was buried underneath. As he searched, something cracked beneath his right knee. Atlas closed his eyes and prayed that he hadn't accidentally discovered the missing transponder. Lifting his knee and moving the papers aside, he realized he'd probably broken what his father had described as the last hope of the Rebellion. He carefully picked up the cracked device, holding it carefully so as not to damage it further.

This transponder looked so different from the others that it had likely been unrecognizable to the P.O.R.T.A.L. soldiers who had torn the lab apart. It had no covering like the other ones and was clearly in the prototype phase. The mechanics, motherboard, microchips and wires were all exposed. Atlas had damaged several of the parts. Of course, he had no idea what they were or how vital they might be to the device's functionality.

Feeling utterly defeated, he placed the broken transponder back on its display and walked upstairs to the cabin. Atlas looked for a place to clean up the dirt and dust from the mines. Surprisingly, there was no sign of running water, and eventually, he gave up.

Atlas sat on the couch and wondered how long it would take to feel confident that P.O.R.T.A.L. was no longer tracking him. He decided that if P.O.R.T.A.L. didn't show up by the next morning, he might be safe and out of harm's way. After eating some scraps of food, he found in the kitchen, Atlas went up to the loft and lay down. Since leaving the mines, he hadn't had a chance to think about Lilou or Nico. He worried that they would suffer the same fate as his father — or worse. The situation felt even more dreadful because the man who killed his mother was the same person who had taken the rest of his family from him. He knew he'd have to do something to rescue his family, but without Element X and his father's transponder, he felt hopeless.

Atlas didn't know when his mind stopped racing or he fell asleep, but before he knew it, the blinding sun came through the window in the loft and woke him. He leaped out of bed and looked over the loft's railing, half expecting to see Allister Craum sitting on the couch, waiting for him. But he was greeted by nothing more than silence and an empty cabin. He wondered if he had disabled the tracker or if, perhaps, he was no longer worth tracking. In either case, he figured it was safe to leave the cabin. He thought about where to go. There was only one option, and one person left to trust. He took the transponder off his neck and typed in the coordinate, Earth B33-Boise, hoping this was precise enough to get him close to his home.

Once through the wormhole, Atlas found himself back in the North End of Boise, standing in the middle of Harrison Boulevard. Atlas turned around, closed the portal, and saw it vanish, only to be replaced by a car speeding toward him, its driver leaning on the horn. Atlas jumped out of the way just in time and landed face-first on the sidewalk. When he stood, he realized he was only ten blocks from home. He turned and started to run.

At the house, he hesitated at the front door. Adora's car was parked on the street. He started to consider what he would say to her. Before he could gather his thoughts, the door was flung open.

"Atlas! You're here! You're alive!" Adora exclaimed. She grabbed him, pulled him inside, and gave him a huge hug. Then she took a step back and held Atlas at arm's length. She looked him over, and then looked over his shoulder. Her voice was anxious. "Where are Lilou and Nico?"

"I don't know," Atlas said sadly.

"What do you mean, you don't know? What happened? Where have you been for the past month? What are you wearing? And why are you covered in dirt?"

"I don't know if you'd believe me if I told you."

"Atlas, come in and sit. And start from the beginning. I want to know everything."

Atlas followed his mom to the dining room table and took a seat next to her. Adora scooted her chair closer to him and patted his knee.

Atlas said, "Do you remember when I told you I wanted to find my father?"

Adora frowned. "Of course, I remember. Atlas, what does that have to do with this?"

"Well, the next day — the day after our fight, we left school to go looking for him."

"Looking for him where?"

Atlas was unsure how honest he should be. He responded, "Boise ... Boise, Idaho."

"Boise? You have been here the whole time?"

"Well, not exactly ..."

"Why didn't you come home?"

"My father ... he made us believe that we could find him."

"You spoke to your father?"

"Yes. Well, sort of. We eventually met him, but we also ran into some terrible people, and now I don't know where Lilou and Nico are," he said. He stared down at his hands.

"Atlas, this is terrible. We need to call the police right now, and you need to tell them everything," Adora said, placing both her hands on his shoulders.

Atlas knew the police couldn't help, but he wondered if he would find relief by telling the truth and getting everything off his chest.

Adora pulled out her cell phone and dialed a pre-programmed number from its phone book. When the other line picked up, she said, "Yes, Detective Brown, it's Adora again. My son Atlas is home, but Lilou and Nico are still missing. Can you come by the house as soon as you can?"

She stood and walked to the kitchen in order to listen to the response in private. When she returned to the dining room, she had hung up and was carrying a glass of water. "Atlas, Detective Brown is coming over. He is the detective assigned to you and your siblings' missing person cases. When he gets here, you need to tell him everything.

"Atlas, look at me. We will get through this, as a family, do you hear me? We will find your brother and sister," Adora said, putting the glass of water on the table in front of him.

Atlas looked at the water and noticed something odd about its behavior. The water in the glass didn't appear level. Instead, the waterline was significantly higher on the side of the cup closest to him — as if it was being pulled toward him.

Adora looked Atlas up and down. "Atlas, you're dirty. Why don't you go upstairs and take a shower and change into some regular clothes before the detective gets here? It might help you feel better."

Atlas realized he was still covered head to toe with the dirt from the mines. As he examined the dirt on his skin more closely, he saw tiny black specs all over that he hadn't noticed before. Suddenly, he remembered what his father had said about Element X back in the lab. "Even the smallest amount would be more than enough to power my new transponder," Atlas mumbled.

"The smallest amount of what? Atlas, what are you talking about?"

Atlas looked up, realizing that Adora had overhead him. "I need to go," he said.

"Go where?"

"I know where Lilou and Nico are. The police can't help us. Only I can save them."

He stood and ran upstairs to his bedroom. There, he quickly changed clothes and searched for a container to hold the dirt from the mines. Adora was shouting at him from downstairs when he spotted a small vial of sand, he'd gotten from a souvenir shop in San Diego just before they'd moved.

Atlas emptied the sand onto the floor and started scraping as much dirt off his body and his discarded clothes as he could into the vial. He held up the vial to see how much he'd collected, but it was only about a quarter full. He hoped it would be enough. He gave the vial a few shakes and noticed that the black specs started to collect toward the bottom. He placed the vial in the back pocket of his pants and ran out of the room. He stopped at the top of the stairs. Adora was at the bottom, waiting for him.

"Atlas, what do you mean only you can save them? You said you didn't know where they were. Please, come down here. The detective will be here soon," Adora said, distressed.

Atlas suddenly remembered their fight. "Listen, I'm sorry about what I said the day before I left. I didn't mean it. I love you, and I love Lilou and Nico. That's why I need to save them. I will find them and bring them back home. I promise." Atlas ran down the stairs past Adora and sprinted toward the garage.

He grabbed his bike and headed out the side door. Adora tried to follow him, but Atlas was on the street, biking toward Boise State University, before she reached the driveway.

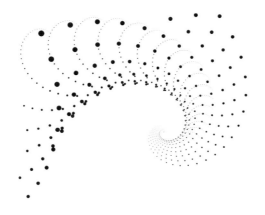

Chapter 16

Atlas furiously pedaled toward the university, heading for Dr. Faraday's office. Without his father's help and Nico's intuition, there was only one person who could help him finish his father's transponder. And as far as he knew, that person was teaching art history at Boise State. Atlas secured the bike, then ran up the stairs to the second floor and Room 208.

He barged into the room. "Dr. Faraday, I need your help!"

Atlas froze, realizing the room was almost entirely empty. The books that had covered the shelves were gone, as were the pictures on the wall. There were only a few items in a box on the desk in the middle of the room. Even the couch he and Lilou and Nico had sat on had been removed.

He's gone ...

As Atlas turned to leave, a voice from the hallway behind him said, "Can I help you with something?" Faraday was standing just outside the office door.

It was strange seeing him, knowing that the professor was his father's doppelganger. The resemblance was there, especially in the eyes, but Faraday was clean shaven and had neatly trimmed hair. He was again wearing thick square-framed glasses and a blue button-down shirt tucked into khaki shorts. "You're still here," Atlas said.

"Atlas, is that you? What are you doing here?"

"I need your help."

"With what? Is this about your father again? Like I said before, kid, I don't know who he is, and I can't help you find him."

"It's not just about my father — they took Lilou and Nico too."

"Who took them?" Faraday looked concerned.

"The same people who have my father. I need your help to get them all back."

"If that's true, you should call the police," Faraday said, reaching into his pocket for his cell phone.

"The police can't help me. My brother and sister aren't here." Atlas hesitated, and then blurted out in frustration, "This is about wormholes, realms, and interdimensional travel. You're the only one who can help!" He felt relieved to finally say what he needed to.

Faraday scanned the hall, then stepped into the office and closed the door. "Everything you told me that day was true, wasn't it?" Faraday said.

"Yes. It was my father who appeared to us that morning through a wormhole. My siblings and I found him, but we also ran into some dangerous people, who captured them. I'm afraid something horrible will happen to them."

"Start from the beginning. How did you find your father?"

"We used one of these." Atlas took one of the transponders off his neck and handed it Faraday, who stared at it intently.

"Is this what I think it is?"

"It's called a transponder, and it can open wormholes to other realms. It's what Lilou, Nico, and I used to track down my father."

"I've seen one of these before, in a dream, a long time ago," Faraday said, a faraway look in his eyes.

"That's because my father, Elio, was secretly communicating with you through a device he called a voice transponder. He was trying to help you finish your research on wormholes. He believed that you were someone ... special. Someone who would be able to finish the work he had started. That's why he sent us to you that day, and why I've come back to you," Atlas said. He paused to take a breath. "Before my father was captured, he was working on a new transponder, one that's more accurate than this one, and I need your help to finish it so that I can rescue everyone from P.O.R.T.A.L."

"Wait, what's P.O.R.T.A.L.?"

"They are the Protectors of Realm Transportation And Logistics. They work for someone — or something — called the Council. They're evil. They want to control the Multiverse."

Faraday thought this over. "You know, the day after you and your siblings came to my office I marched down to the Dean's office and resigned from the art department. Then I convinced him to hire me as the new Professor of Theoretical Physics for Boise State. That's why my office is empty. Today I'm moving my things into my new laboratory."

"What made you resign as art professor?"

"You did, Atlas. You and your siblings revived my passion for science and physics. Actually, I wasn't sure

I believed what you told me that day; but I believe you now. I promise. I will help you finish your father's transponder. Come on, I'll show you my new lab, and you can show me how that transponder works."

Faraday grabbed the last box off the desk. Atlas followed him to the elevator. The professor seemed happier and more confident than he had four and a half weeks ago. "Say, did your brother take my book that day? I couldn't find it when I packed up."

"Maybe, I'll have to take a look around for it," Atlas replied vaguely.

As they walked to the science building, Faraday explained how he'd convinced the Dean to open a new school within the university's School of Science. He also mentioned that he'd received a large grant for his new state-of-the-art lab.

Faraday flung open the big double doors to the underground lab. "Here it is."

Atlas looked shocked. "It's ... empty," he said.

"Of course, it's empty. I just got the grant. I haven't had time to buy any equipment. But look at all the space. It's even bigger than my lab back in Stanford," Faraday replied, placing the box on a large worktable in the center of the room. The professor closed and locked the double doors. "I believe you have something you wanted to show me?"

"Right. The transponder." Atlas took it off his neck and handed it to Faraday. "Press the button on the back to turn it on," Atlas said.

As soon as Faraday did, the transponder began emitting the holographic image of the Multiverse. Faraday stared at the image in wonder. "I've seen this map before, also in a dream. It's a map of the Multiverse, isn't it?"

"Yes, and the device works like you thought it would. It emits quantum frequencies that vibrate cosmic strings, opening wormholes in spacetime. This one belongs to my father. It's programmed with every known realm in the Multiverse."

"But how can this small device produce the energy needed to open a wormhole?"

"My father said it uses a quantum reactor."

"Of course. Unfortunately, we're years away from developing such a reactor ourselves, but I could use this transponder, or one like it, to reverse-engineer the reactor," Faraday said. "Now, where is this other transponder you mentioned, the one your father was working on?"

"It's not here. I left it back in my father's lab … but we can use that transponder to get it." Atlas took the transponder from the professor and entered the coordinate Elena into its interface. The space in front of Faraday immediately ripped open, revealing an iridescent portal.

Faraday stared at it in awe. "It looks exactly how I imagined it would. Is it safe?" he asked.

Atlas nodded and stepped through the portal, knowing Faraday would follow.

On the other side, Atlas turned to watch Faraday emerge. He could almost see the scientist's silhouette through the portal. It reminded him of his father in Lilou's bedroom.

"Where are we?" Faraday said, stepping through the portal and taking in his new surroundings.

"This realm is called Elena, it's an uncharted realm ... or at least it was," Atlas replied, realizing that it was now likely on P.O.R.T.A.L.'s radar. "It was named after my mother," he added.

"Your mother?"

"My birth mother. She was murdered by a man named Allister Craum, the man who now has Lilou, Nico, and my father."

"I'm so sorry to hear about your mother. Don't worry. We will get them back." Faraday put an arm around Atlas's shoulder. "Now, take me to your father's lab."

"I think his cabin is further up the mountain."

They hiked up through the trees until Atlas spotted the cabin. "There it is," he said, pointing.

"Your father lived there?"

"For twelve years. He was hiding from Allister Craum and P.O.R.T.A.L. while he worked on his transponder. He believed it would save the Rebellion."

"The Rebellion? You mean war?"

Atlas stopped before opening the door. "Yes, but we're only here to get Lilou and Nico back."

"And your father?"

"Yes. Him too. Come on. The entrance to the lab is just over there," Atlas said, leading Faraday to the trap door and down the stairs. Atlas scanned the lab to make sure everything was exactly how he'd left it. To his relief, his father's transponder was still on its display.

"What happened here?" Faraday asked.

"P.O.R.T.A.L happened. This is where they captured my father." Atlas stepped over the mess and took the transponder off its display. "We need to go," he said. "I left the wormhole in the woods open so that we could return directly to your lab."

They climbed upstairs and headed for the front door. As they did, Atlas saw something out of the corner of his eye that stopped him cold. On a small table near the cabin's entrance was a small picture frame that held a photo of a woman standing in the middle of a city, one he now recognized. He picked up the frame and took out the photo. It was the other half of the torn picture of his father from the shoe box.

Atlas looked closely at the woman. "Adora ... is my mother?" he whispered.

Faraday looked over Atlas's shoulder. "Your mother is beautiful, kid. But I thought you said her name was Elena."

"It is. My real mother's name was Elena, but my adoptive mother's name is Adora. And it looks like they're the same person," Atlas said, clutching the photo.

"I'm sorry, kid, I'm still new to this. You're going to have to elaborate."

"The Multiverse is made up of billions of Earths, many of which are almost identical to ours," Atlas said. "That means we all have doppelgangers. In fact — you're my father's doppelganger, and now I've discovered that Adora is my mother's doppelganger."

"Wait ... you're saying I look identical to your father?"

"Well, not exactly. You two don't dress or act anything alike. He also has a lot more hair and he's a bit rounder. But yes; you're his doppelganger."

"But how did I not recognize myself in the picture that day in my office?" Faraday looked perplexed. "I guess I didn't look very close."

"Don't worry. I didn't make the connection at first either."

"So, you didn't know that your adoptive mother is your birth mother's doppelganger?"

"I had no idea until this moment."

"What does it mean?"

"I don't know what it means. But we need to get back to your lab." Atlas put the photo in his back pocket. He led Faraday out of the cabin and back the way they'd come.

As they walked down the mountain, Atlas took one last look at his father's cabin, knowing it might be his last. Elio had said his mother wanted to raise Atlas here. For a moment, he imagined being rocked by his mother on the porch swing. He pictured his mother cradling him, keeping him warm and close to her. In his mind's eye, he saw his father stepping outside to join his mother, before leaning in for a kiss and sharing a moment as they stared into their precious child's eyes. Just as he was picturing his infant-self reaching for his mother's finger, he was snapped back to reality.

"Atlas, what are you staring at? Let's get back to my lab," Faraday called to him from further down the mountain.

Atlas quickly caught up with him, and they walked back through the portal together.

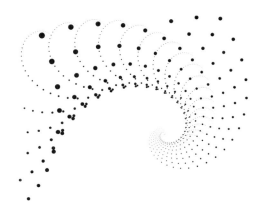

Chapter 17

"That was extraordinary!" Faraday said, taking a seat at the big worktable.

Atlas hadn't had a chance to think about how miraculous the technology was. "It is amazing, isn't it?"

"Now, let me see this thing."

Atlas sat across from Faraday and carefully handed him the device.

Faraday held up the transponder and looked at it from all angles. "It looks broken. I thought you needed my help to finish this, not fix it."

"If it helps, before I broke it, all it needed was this," Atlas said, taking the vial of Element X out of his back pocket.

"And what exactly is that?"

"This is Element X. My father said even the tiniest amount of it would be enough to power his transponder. He believed it's a form of dark matter that emits something he called dark energy. If all that's true, it's the only thing strong enough to power the new transponder."

"Dark matter, huh? It looks like dirt to me," Faraday said, picking up the vial and gently shaking it.

"Is this table level?" Atlas asked.

"I believe so, why?"

"Do you have something round, like a ball, or anything that can roll?"

"Sure, look in that box from my office. I think there's a small globe in it. What's this about?" he asked. His eyes remained fixed on the vial.

Atlas dug through the box for the globe and found it at the very bottom.

"Okay, now place the vial on the table in front of you," Atlas directed. He took the globe and put it on the table across from Faraday. The moment the globe left his hand, it rolled toward the vial and knocked it over before rolling off the table.

"Okay. I'm intrigued, but perhaps this table is uneven." Faraday checked under the table to see if all the legs were flat to the ground.

"It's not the table," Atlas said. "Toss me the vial, and you place the globe on the table."

They reversed the experiment. Faraday picked up the globe and vial. He slid the latter across to Atlas, then released the globe. Once again, it rolled straight toward the vial, knocking it over. This time, Atlas stopped the objects before they fell off the table.

"That's extraordinary. The dirt appears to be producing a large gravitational pull, especially for its size," Faraday said. "Did you say it's also emitting some sort of dark energy?"

"Yes, why?"

Faraday got up and stood on top of the table. "My turn to conduct an experiment." He detached a fluorescent light from one of the panels above the worktable. "Atlas, please flip the light switches on the wall."

Atlas, unsure of what Faraday was trying to prove, got up and flipped all the lights off. But the lights didn't go off; they only dimmed slightly. Similarly, the fluorescent light in Faraday's hand remained on. The scientist moved the light toward the vial on the table. This caused the light glow more brightly. He continued to move the light toward the vial until it burst in his hands.

"Atlas, this is amazing. I've never seen anything like this," Faraday said. "Where did you find such a thing?"

"It's a long story, but we found it in a mine controlled by P.O.R.T.A.L.," Atlas replied, turning the lights back on.

Faraday grabbed a broom and a dustpan from the closet and cleaned up the broken light.

"So, can you fix it?" Atlas said.

"I don't know, kid. I'll need to get some computers and equipment here, and I'll need *both* of your transponders." Faraday nodded toward the transponders around Atlas's neck.

"What do you need these for?"

"I assume that the technology in them is similar to the technology in this one. The only way to figure out what has been damaged is to take those transponders apart."

"Why do you need them both? They're the only ones I have. What if you fail?"

"All of these transponders are different sizes and shapes, which means their technology is not identical. I'll need to disassemble them and compare their parts. I may also need to borrow some parts from one or both of them to make your father's new transponder whole again."

Atlas hesitated, realizing that the transponders were his only connections with the Multiverse. At the same time, he knew that without his father's new transponder, he'd have no chance of saving his brother, sister, and father. He had to accept the risk.

Atlas reluctantly pulled the transponders off his neck and slid them across the table. "Here. And you might need this too," he said, taking the voice transponder out of his ear and placing it on the table.

"What's that? It looks like a Bluetooth headset."

"It's a voice transponder. You use it to communicate by tapping into a person's life-frequency. It's how Elio found me, and how he secretly shared his information with you all those years. I don't know exactly how it works, but I know my father incorporated the technology from that into his new transponder."

"Thank you, Atlas. I know you're putting a lot of trust in me, and I promise to take good care of these. Now, it's getting late. I don't know if you planned on going home, but I'll be working through the night. You're more than welcome to crash on the couch."

Atlas nodded and walked over to the couch he and his siblings had sat on when they first met Faraday. He lay and thought about everything that had happened since that time, and everything he'd learned. He was almost afraid to think too deeply about Lilou and Nico. He was afraid of what would happen to them if he didn't rescue them soon. Atlas knew that Elio would immediately be sent to Purgatory, which Mia had described as like being trapped in a wormhole for eternity. He prayed that he could rescue his siblings before they suffered the same fate.

Atlas thought about Adora and her connection with his birth mother. Although he'd been surprised seeing the photo, he also felt an overwhelming sense of comfort in the discovery. Although he knew Elena and Adora were not the same person, he pondered the chances of his mother's doppelganger being the person who adopted him. He'd never known the full story of his adoption. One day, his foster parents told him he was being adopted and should be happy to finally have a real family. He desperately wanted to run home and ask Adora about his adoption. But he couldn't return there without Lilou and Nico by his side.

***

Atlas woke up the next morning to the sound of Faraday wheeling a large black box into the lab on a dolly. He noticed that the professor had already moved in several large pieces of equipment, including several computers. "Where did you get all this?" Atlas said.

"I borrowed them — most from the science department, like those computers and those 3-D printers over there. Some of it, like the welding tools, I took from the engineering department. Don't worry; we'll return it all when we're done."

"What about that?" Atlas pointed at the black box.

"Oh, this. This is a quantum computer. It's one hundred million times faster than a traditional computer. We'll need to return it before the weekend ends. If anyone notices it's missing, we'll be in big trouble."

Atlas helped Faraday move and set up the new equipment. By the time they'd finished, over an hour later, the big open room was beginning to look more like a laboratory.

"Were you able to figure anything out last night?" Atlas saw that all three transponders were sitting on the large worktable, disassembled. He felt chilled at the thought of never being able to open a wormhole again.

"Ah, yes, congratulations!" Faraday said. "From what I can see, you did put a crack in the quantum reactor. I can't just borrow a quantum reactor from one of the other transponders, because they're all different. I'll need to rebuild your father's transponder from the ground up. Also, it looks like you broke the hologram emitter, so I'll need to give the device an entirely new interface as well." He looked extremely cheerful.

"When do you think it will be finished?"

"With your help, I believe we can get it done today."

With Faraday's guidance, Atlas helped print new parts and weld small pieces together. Once the physical device was finished, Faraday used the quantum computer to program the device's new interface. Finally, all that was left was to add particles of Element X into the device's rebuilt quantum reactor.

At the end of the day, Faraday held up the finished transponder. "There. It's done!" he exclaimed.

"It looks like a cell phone ..."

"It's supposed to. I wanted to build an interface you'd be more familiar with," Faraday said. "Go ahead, turn it on."

Atlas took the transponder and pushed a small button on the device's side. Instead of emitting a holographic map of the Multiverse, the map appeared on the transponder's rectangular screen. "What's this blue dot?" Atlas asked.

"I input the frequencies from your voice transponder into this transponder computer, but I don't know who that frequency belongs to," Faraday explained.

It's Mia, Atlas thought. "But wait, there should be two more. Where are Lilou and Nico's signatures?" he said, his hands suddenly clammy.

"I don't know, kid, but if they were there, you could travel straight to them. You know, maybe there was an issue in the uploading process, let me try again," Faraday said, reaching for the transponder.

Atlas pulled it away, certain that was not the issue. "They must have already been sent to Purgatory. It's too late," he said despondently.

"So they're not dead?"

"No. Purgatory is like an eternal prison. My friend Mia said that nobody has ever come out of it alive."

"But if they're not dead, there's still hope. If you can get inside, maybe there's a way to release them."

"I don't know if that's possible. Even if I could, Purgatory is in one of P.O.R.T.A.L.'s central hubs guarded by hundreds of soldiers — and him."

"Who is him?"

"Allister Craum," Atlas said, collapsing into a chair.

Faraday recalled that Craum was the man who had murdered Atlas's mother. "Atlas, I think I know how you can break into that place and free your brother and sister. Just give me a second, they're almost finished," he said, walking over to the 3-D printers.

With all the noise and other distractions in the lab, Atlas hadn't noticed that Faraday was printing something. He watched intently as the professor picked up two objects from the printers. He then inserted two other small devices that looked like small flashlights into the objects before returning to the table.

"I wasn't sure you would need these, but here they are," he said, holding up the two objects.

"Why do they look like ray-guns?" Atlas asked.

"Well, I took some creative liberty with the design, but no, they're not ray-guns. I call them portal-casters."

"Portal-casters ...?"

"I wanted to avoid using the term "gun." Is that a problem?"

"No, they're great," Atlas conceded, inspecting them.

About the size of a standard pistol, the portal-casters were made of glossy white plastic. Each one had an angled grip and a trigger guard that protected a small red button. Aside from the button, the devices had no mechanics or movable parts. In place of a barrel was a small infrared light, which Faraday had inserted into the 3-D printed mold. The light was activated by pressing the red button.

"What's this inscription on the side of the guns?" Atlas asked, squinting his eyes.

"It says: *The courage of the few, decide the fate of the many.* We had it inscribed on the wall in our Stanford lab as inspiration for the work we were doing. I always thought I'd come up with it, but I'm starting to think that maybe your father slipped the idea to me while I was sleeping," Faraday said with a half wink.

"So, what do they do?"

"Right, of course. It's simple. Each of these is just a 3-D printed mold. The small infrared device I placed inside connects directly to your transponder. Just point the beam at any surface, press the button, and your transponder will use triangulation to open a portal at that exact location. Then you take the other caster and point it at another surface, and your transponder will open a second portal, thus completing the wormhole. Come on; let's give it a shot," Faraday said.

Atlas examined the portal-casters more closely. "So, all I do is point and shoot and I can open a wormhole anywhere?" Atlas wondered if this was what Elio had meant by using wormholes strategically on the battlefield.

"Exactly." Faraday said.

Atlas extended one arm and pointed the casters at the wall across from him. He pressed the button. A portal appeared on the wall. Atlas turned around, pointed the other caster at the wall behind him and pressed the other button. Instantly, another portal appeared, on the opposite wall from the first. Both portals were translucent and iridescent, like every other portal he had traveled through.

"Did it work?" Atlas asked. He remembered his father mentioning issues with the wormhole's stability.

"There's only one way to find out."

Atlas was about to walk through the first portal when Faraday stopped him, panicked. "What are you doing? You don't want to test it like that. I meant, throw something through it."

"Oh ... right," Atlas said, embarrassed. He grabbed the small globe off the table and tossed it through the first portal. It immediately bounced off the floor behind him on the other side of the room.

"I guess that means it works. All right, it's safe to walk through now," Faraday said, motioning for Atlas to give it a try.

Atlas nodded, slowly stepped through, and immediately found himself on the other side of the room. He turned and walked back through the portal, ending up where he'd started. "How do you close the portals?" he asked.

"Press both buttons again, and they should close."

"Do you think I can use these to break into one of P.O.R.T.A.L.'s hubs, get past the soldiers, and rescue everybody?"

"Whoa! Not so fast, kid. You're going to need a bit more practice before you rescue your family." Faraday grinned. "But don't worry, I know just the place." He grabbed his coat and car keys and bounded out the double doors.

Atlas quickly stuffed the transponder in his pocket and tucked the two portal-casters into his belt before following Faraday. They walked out of the science building and toward the parking lot and Faraday's car. Atlas noticed the sun had begun to set. He wondered where the professor could be taking him.

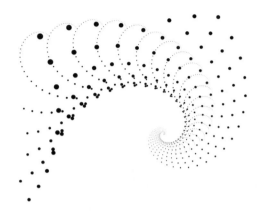

Chapter 18

"Where are we headed?" Atlas asked from the passenger seat.

"You'll see. It's just a ten-minute drive down the road," Faraday replied.

They drove in silence as they went up Broadway Avenue, over the freeway, and past the airport. As the sun set over the horizon, they reached an industrial-looking building on the outskirts of town. The parking lot was deserted. Faraday hopped out of the car and opened the trunk.

Atlas got out and looked at him quizzically. "What is this place?"

"An indoor paintball park." Faraday held a paintball gun in one hand and a mask in the other. "It's a little hobby of mine. I come here most weekends to blow off steam," he said, slamming the trunk shut. "And it's great exercise," he added.

Atlas realized he didn't know much about Faraday besides his background in quantum and theoretical physics. Was he married? Did he have kids? But this wasn't the right time to ask. Instead, he said, "How will we get in? There's nobody here, and it looks closed."

"If you can't get into this place, how exactly do you plan on rescuing your family?" Faraday responded before walking off, paintball gun in hand.

Atlas realized Faraday was right. To get his family back, he'd have to use his portal-casters, and also take risks. He followed Faraday to the building.

"If I remember correctly, the main paintball course should be just behind this wall," Faraday said.

"How are we getting inside?"

"Why don't you try casting a portal on that wall there?"

"Sure. But where do I open the other portal?"

"I don't think we'll need another door. If we walk through the single door, we should end up on the other side of that wall."

Atlas released one of the casters from his belt, pointed it at the wall, and pressed the button to open a portal. Like the other portals, it was slightly transparent, exposing the inside of the building and giving him confidence that this would work. He glanced at Faraday for reassurance, then stepped through into the darkened building.

Faraday followed, almost bumping into Atlas. "It worked! Excellent job, Atlas. Now, help me find the light switches."

They gingerly walked to the entrance of the paintball course, then flipped on every light they could find. The building was about the size of a small air plane hangar. Its high ceilings allowed enough space for a few small wooden structures to fit inside. The course was filled with obstacles. There were large and small plywood structures, old, broken-down cars, concrete walls and bunkers, and an assortment of random barrels and boxes intended for players to duck and hide behind.

"What now?" Atlas asked.

"We're going to play a fun little game of Capture the Flag," Faraday said. He smiled, clearly impressed with himself as he stuck a large flagpole into the dirt floor.

"But we've only got one paintball gun."

"I know, kid. That's because you get to use those." Faraday indicated the portal-casters. "Take this mask, go to the other side of the course and get in position," he said, loading his paintball gun. "And if it wasn't obvious, if you get hit with one of my paintballs, you're out."

Atlas realized that "out" in future games would mean death inside of P.O.R.T.A.L.'s Central Hub. He broke into a cold sweat.

He trudged to the other side of the course and tried to both psych himself up and calm his nerves. He scanned the course. From his position behind a big box, he could barely see the flag at the far end, in front of a large concrete barricade. He looked for Faraday, but he'd likely found his own position.

Then he heard Faraday shout, "Game on!"

Atlas cautiously stepped out from behind the box. As he moved toward the bunker in front of him, he was hit with two paintballs to his chest, and another to his face mask.

"Start again! This time, try using your casters!"

Atlas sighed and returned to his starting position.

This time, using his casters, he opened a portal on the wall behind him, and one on the wall to his right, which he stepped through. Once through, he ducked behind some plywood boards. Atlas was confident that if Faraday hadn't spotted his portal, he'd have no clue where he was. Atlas warily poked his head out. Faraday was at the far end of the course, pointing his paintball gun back and forth, looking for him. From his new vantage point, Atlas could no longer see the flag. He'd have to get closer before making his move.

He spotted a small two-story tower about twelve feet high at the center of the course. The tower was roughly ten feet in length and four feet wide. It appeared to be designed to give a referee the ability to see the whole course. He surmised that if he could place a portal just right on the plywood wall of the structure, he could get on the second floor and spot the flag.

He opened a portal on the wall in front of him, aimed his second caster at the tower, and pressed the button. Stepping through the portal, he found himself in the tower. He peeked over the low plywood wall that faced the opposite end of the course and spotted the flag. Faraday must have seen him, because a barrage of paintballs splattered on the front of the tower. This caused Atlas to drop into a prone position.

"That's better! But you're going to need to do even better than that. Your advantage is not your ability to stay hidden, it's your ability to move!" Faraday cried.

Atlas slowly raised his head and peeked over the wall to survey where, on the course, to place portals. This time, instead of trying to move stealthily, he decided he would move fast and keep Faraday's head on a swivel.

On the far side of the tower, there was an opening where the ladder was attached that looked big enough for him to pass through. Atlas got ready to run and jump through the opening.

Faraday shouted, "I know you're still up there. This flag isn't going to catch itself!"

Atlas stood and sprinted toward the opening. As he ran, paintballs chased him, narrowly missing him. Reaching the edge of the tower, he leapt. As he plummeted toward the ground, with the caster in his left hand, he opened a portal behind Faraday on the far wall of the course. Then he aimed his other caster at the ground and pressed the button just before impact. His momentum caused him to fall through the portal on the far wall headfirst, forcing him into a somersault when he hit the ground. He jumped back to his feet and looked for the flag.

The flag was nearby, but he calculated that if he ran for it, he'd be hit with a paintball before reaching it. Instead, he stepped into the open, found Faraday, who was spinning around looking for him, and yelled, "Hey! I'm over here!"

As Faraday turned toward the sound of his voice, Atlas opened a portal on a plywood wall directly behind Faraday. Faraday hesitated. He looked over his left shoulder at the wall, wondering why Atlas would open a portal so close to him, then raised his paintball gun. As Faraday started firing, Atlas opened a second portal on the wall behind himself and stepped through. Once through, he closed the second door and opened a new door on the giant concrete barricade directly behind the flag. He gave Dr. Faraday a quick tap on the shoulder before stepping back through the portal. This placed Atlas in front of the flag. Faraday turned at Atlas's touch, but the portal had closed. When Faraday turned back, Atlas was ten yards in front of him, holding the flag above his head.

"Atlas, that was brilliant. You outsmarted me!" Faraday shouted. He ran over and gave Atlas a high five.

Hearing a compliment from Faraday prompted Atlas to reflect on the time he'd spent with Elio. His birth father had seemed far more interested in Nico's intelligence and intuitions than in establishing a connection with him. Atlas couldn't shake his anger at Elio for admitting that he'd lied about looking for him or his resentment that Elio seemed to express that the loss of his mother, Elena, was Elio's alone.

Atlas raised his hand high above his head to meet Dr. Faraday's high five. For one of the first times, he felt proud of something he had accomplished. "Thank you, Dr. Faraday — for everything," Atlas said with a wide smile.

"No problem, kid. And do me a favor; call me Malcolm from now on. Now let's run it back," he said as he checked the hopper for more paintballs.

He wants to run it back ...

Atlas and Faraday played several more games of capture the flag until Atlas felt fully confident in his ability to use the portal-casters. Exhausted, they drove back to the lab to rest. Atlas felt uncomfortable asking Faraday about his personal life, but it was clear that he probably wasn't married and didn't have kids, because over the past two days in the lab, he'd never made a phone call or checked in with anyone.

***

Atlas woke the next morning on the couch to the sound of Faraday opening the double doors carrying a large box into the lab.

"What's in the box?" he asked, rising from the couch.

"Something I kept from my old lab. I ran home to get it. I hope it fits you." Faraday pulled out what looked like a sleek one-piece garment. A tiny, raised diamond pattern covered the white fabric, giving the material a textured look and feel.

"What is it?"

"It's a body suit made of a special textile. We used these to shield us from radiation. It dawned on me last night that you'll be traveling through more wormholes than the average kid and might need some protection. You'll also need this," Faraday said, pulling out a white helmet that looked similar to a full-faced motorcycle helmet. "It's also designed to protect against radiation. Plus, it has a built-in heads-up display on its visor that I can link to your transponder. Using the transponder's ability to detect and triangulate life-frequencies, it should provide you with a real-time 3-D map of your environment."

"You mean I'll be able to see if an enemy is around a corner or behind a closed door?"

"Precisely."

Within minutes, Faraday had paired the helmet with Atlas's transponder. "That should do it. Go on, try them on," he said, throwing Atlas the suit, followed by the helmet.

Atlas quickly changed into the bodysuit and helmet, then holstered his transponders and casters into the tactical belt Dr. Faraday had obviously designed overnight to hold his devices.

"Hey, look at that. It fits you perfectly," Faraday said with a broad smile.

Atlas smiled back. "Thanks again," he said.

"No problem, kid. Consider it an early birthday gift."

"Wait … What's the date?" Atlas realized he'd lost track of time since he'd left home, now almost five weeks ago.

"It's October second, I believe. Why?"

"Yesterday was my thirteenth birthday ..."

"Your birthday? That's wonderful. Then I guess you can consider it a late birthday gift," Faraday said, his smile widening.

But Atlas was frowning.

"What's wrong, kid?"

"I don't know if I'm ready. What if I can't get them back?"

"Look, I don't know exactly what you're up against, but after what I saw yesterday, I know ..." Faraday started to say, when they heard a knock at the door. "That's strange. I didn't think anyone else was in the building. Wait here. I'll see who it is." Faraday walked to the door and opened it half-way. "Yes, can I help you?"

"My name is Detective Brown, and I'm investigating the case of a missing child," said a man with a deep voice.

Atlas, recognizing the name, ducked under the table, and crawled toward the back, away from the door.

"Is there something specific I can help you with, detective?" Faraday replied calmly.

"I found the missing child's bike here on campus. I also noticed that your car is one of the few parked in the lot. I talked to one of the janitors. He said he thinks your car has been here all weekend. Is that true?"

"Yes. I've been here setting up my new lab. I'm trying to get everything squared away before school tomorrow. I'm sorry. What does this have to do with me?" Faraday replied in a polite tone.

"I was thinking you might have seen the kid since you've been on campus all weekend. Do you mind if I come in? I'd like to show you a picture of him," the detective asked.

Faraday glanced over his shoulder. Atlas was nowhere in sight. "Look, I'm really swamped, and I haven't seen any kids around here."

"It will only take a minute, I promise," the detective insisted.

Faraday took one last look around the room but didn't see Atlas, so he reluctantly answered, "Sure. Come on in, detective."

Brown surveyed the lab, looking at every corner.

"I thought you had a photo you wanted to show me?" Faraday said.

"Oh, I'm sorry, here it is." Brown handed him a photograph of Atlas.

Faraday pretended to analyze the image. "Hmm. Sorry, I haven't seen this kid on campus. As I said, I've mostly been here in this lab."

"Well, here's the thing, Mr. Faraday," the detective said, "his mother says that about a month ago, the day before the kid went missing, he came to campus looking for you." Brown suddenly stooped down to see if anyone was hiding under the desk.

Faraday ducked his head under the opposite side of the table, only to find himself face-to-face with Brown. Both men stood and eyed each other suspiciously. Faraday said, "As I said, detective, I've never met that boy, and I don't know why he'd come here looking for me, do you?"

Brown sighed. "Do me a favor. Keep that photo and keep your eye out for him. Call me if you have any information at all or remember anything out of the ordinary." The detective handed Faraday his business card and left.

As soon as Faraday was alone, he circled through the lab but found no trace of Atlas. It dawned on him: There was only one way Atlas could have gotten out of the room undetected. Smirking, Faraday whispered to himself, "Good luck, kid."

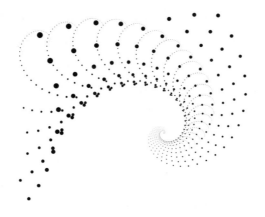

Chapter 19

When Atlas, under the table, heard the detective enter the lab, he knew he had to get out of there. While the door was closing, he used his casters to open a portal to the outside of the lab, and one directly at his feet. The moment the door closed behind the detective, Atlas entered the wormhole and found himself outside the lab. He closed both portals and dropped his head below the door's window. Wanting to know what the detective had to say, Atlas cautiously raised his head and peeked through the door's blinds.

Although it was hard to make out the conversation, he did hear Brown say something about Adora leading him here and saw both men look for him beneath the table. He knew he could no longer stay at the lab. It was time for him to save his family.

He ducked around a corner, pulled his transponder off his belt, and opened a wormhole to realm Uncharted 5. Without hesitation, he stepped through and was back in the prehistoric realm Elio had used to avoid detection. Atlas surveyed his surroundings. Seeing a large carnivorous dinosaur standing rather too close for comfort, he promptly closed the wormhole behind him and opened a new one to Earth A14-Boise, the realm and city in which he believed he'd find Lilou, Nico, and hopefully, his father.

Atlas found himself in a familiar place on the outskirts of the city, near a small farmhouse and right next to a large red barn. He remembered P.O.R.T.A.L. had taken mere minutes to track him the first time he and his siblings arrived. He'd have to hurry to avoid capture. In the distance, Atlas saw the giant neon sign that read "WELCOME TO BOISE" floating in the sky, just outside the city. He opened a portal on the broad side of the barn and a second one on the floating sign. Emerging on the other side, he fell a short distance and landed on the sign's metal railing.

He stood and admired the skyline that was now right in front of him. Towering high above the other skyscrapers, Atlas spied P.O.R.T.A.L.'s Central Hub. He wondered how many hubs P.O.R.T.A.L. had across the Multiverse. Did each realm have only one? Or could these hubs be found in every major city in the known System?

As he stared at the city in wonder, Atlas remembered the torn photograph of his parents. It dawned on him: This was the realm they were originally from. It was the only explanation for why someone had written the coordinates on the note in his mother's things. It also explained the photo of Elio and Elena standing in the city streets. The photo must have been taken before P.O.R.T.A.L. arrived.

Within minutes, Atlas saw several transports leaving the city, heading toward the farmhouse. He knew they were looking for him, so he waited until he saw the ships complete their search and return to the city before making his next move.

Okay, Atlas thought. *I need to get inside that building and get to the top. That's where I'll find Purgatory, along with Lilou, Nico, and my father.*

Atlas decided to try to stay as high as possible to avoid being seen. He carefully aimed a caster at the highest rooftop he could see and opened a portal. Once on that rooftop, he portal-jumped from rooftop to rooftop until he reached the top of the building adjacent to P.O.R.T.A.L.'s Central Hub.

Atlas crept to the rooftop's edge and stood on its ledge, looking up at the ominous structure in front of him. From the outside, the giant building looked like one solid edifice without windows, or any other means to see inside. Atlas tried to look inside using his transponder but saw only static on his screen where the building should have been. That's when he remembered what Elio had said about P.O.R.T.A.L.'s hub having a state-of-the-art jamming system. It must have been disrupting his transponder's ability to create a real-time 3-D map of the building.

Atlas gave a resigned shrug. *I guess I'll have to go in blind,* he thought.

Looking down, he saw that the gap between the buildings was relatively small; a narrow alleyway divided them. He figured if he got a decent running start, he could jump off his rooftop and reach the building on the other side. Atlas looked back down at the gap he'd have to clear, then stepped back until he felt he was far enough away to reach full speed.

Once in position, he pulled out a caster and held it at his side. He ran until he was in a full sprint and jumped off the rooftop. As he fell toward the Hub, he pointed the caster at the wall and pressed the button at the last second, allowing him to fall through the portal and into the building's interior.

Atlas hit the floor and gracelessly tumbled head over heels until he came to a stop. He slowly climbed to his feet, hoping he hadn't broken any bones. He was in a room filled with workers dressed in long white lab coats. The room was large with high ceilings. Giant screens on the walls displayed maps of the Multiverse. Perhaps P.O.R.T.A.L. used the room to monitor the System.

Every worker in the room immediately stopped and stared at the boy who had fallen through a solid wall in a strange bodysuit and helmet. After a few moments of awkward silence, a worker nonchalantly walked over to a computer attached to a wall and pressed a large red button. Immediately, an alarm blared throughout the building.

Well, there goes the element of surprise, Atlas thought, worried that he'd just made a critical error. The workers near him raised their hands above their heads at the sight of Atlas's portal-casters. Those further away scrambled out of the room.

Atlas realized that now that he was inside the building, the jamming system was no longer interfering with his transponder. He could now access the real-time 3-D map of the building. Looking at his visor's screen, he could see the life-frequencies of every person in the room, as well as those in the building's surrounding areas, displayed as tiny red dots. Not all of the dots were moving away from him. From the corridor outside the room, two blinking red dots were closing in fast on his position.

Here they come, he thought, pulling out his second caster.

As the soldiers turned the corner, one of them pointed his rifle at Atlas, and shouted, "Drop your weapons and place your hands above your head, now!"

Atlas knew that if he did so, it would all be over. He carefully raised his casters above his head, betting the soldiers would issue another warning before discharging their weapons. Once the casters were above his head, he pointed one at the ceiling and pressed the button.

"I said, drop your weapons!" the soldier repeated, as both slowly started to approach him.

Atlas stood frozen, both his hands high above his head, trying not to appear threatening. As the soldiers came nearer, a worker running from the room tripped over a desk. When the soldiers took their eyes off Atlas for a split second, Atlas pointed his second caster at their feet and pressed the button. They fell through the floor and then down through the ceiling. Looking up in anticipation, Atlas almost forgot to jump away to avoid being crushed by their falling bodies. As they slammed into the floor behind him, Atlas ran for the exit.

Once outside the room and inside the building's maze of corridors, Atlas saw four more red dots on his heads-up display. They seemed to be descending, in what he assumed to be the building's elevator system. Although Atlas knew it was risky to head toward the soldiers, he also knew it was likely his fastest route to the top of the building. He turned the next corner and headed for the elevator.

When Atlas reached the elevator's corridor, he stopped at the opposite end and waited for it to open. With one caster, he opened a portal on the wall next to him. When the elevator door opened, he pointed the second caster over the soldiers' shoulders and opened a portal on the back wall of the elevator. The soldiers, oblivious to the portal, came rushing out of the elevator firing their energy rifles down the corridor at Atlas, clearly having been ordered to shoot on sight. Dodging the energy pulses, Atlas jumped through the portal next to him and landed in the empty elevator behind the soldiers. Atlas watched the soldiers point their rifles back and forth, befuddled. How could he have disappeared in front of their eyes? One soldier turned and caught a glimpse of Atlas as the elevator door closed. He shouted, "He's in the elevator!"

Atlas breathed a sigh of relief before pressing the top button on the elevator's digital display, assuming it would take him to the top of the building. As he began his ascent, he pulled out his transponder to see if he could zoom out, because he hadn't had a chance to explore the map of the building. That's when he saw Lilou and Nico's blue life-frequencies blinking in the room he remembered was labeled Purgatory.

That's right. The building's jamming system blocked their frequencies from being detected when I was on the outside. But if I can see their life-frequencies now, they must not have been sent into Purgatory — yet, Atlas thought, relieved.

He activated his voice transponder. "Lilou, are you there, can you hear me?"

Atlas, is that really you? she gasped.

"Yes, I'm here, inside the building. Is Nico with you?"

Yes, he's here with me. Wait, what do you mean, you're inside the building?

"Thank heaven you guys are okay. I was worried they'd sent you to Purgatory. I came to rescue you."

Atlas, we're in some kind of holding cell. They've scheduled us to be sent to Purgatory in fifteen minutes. You must hurry!

"Nico, can you hear me? What happened to my father?" Atlas said, connecting Nico to their transmission.

Atlas, I'm here. I'm sorry, but they sent Elio to Purgatory yesterday. Purgatory is like nothing we've encountered before. It's similar to your father's transponder in that it creates a new wormhole, but from what I've observed, it requires an enormous amount of energy. The machine uses a massive quantum reactor, which slows time, allowing them to open and close both portal-doors simultaneously, trapping the person inside the wormhole. But the machine has a flaw. The core of the reactor has to recharge after each use, only allowing them to open Purgatory once per day.

Now that he could detect their life-frequencies, Atlas knew he could use his transponder to travel directly to his siblings, but it was too risky without knowing who else was in the room. He decided to stick to his plan. "Nico, don't worry, I'm on my way. I'm in the elevator now, heading to the top floor," he said.

Atlas, please be careful. He is here, Lilou said.

She didn't have to say his name. Atlas knew that to rescue his brother and sister, he'd have to confront Allister Craum. Atlas saw a cluster of red dots on his heads-up display gathering outside an elevator door above him. "'Lilou, Nico, I need to go. I've run into some trouble. I'll be there as soon as I can," Atlas said.

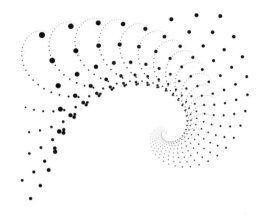

Chapter 20

A tlas knew he'd be caught the instant the elevator door opened. He frantically pressed the buttons on the elevator's digital display, hoping to stop it before it reached the top floor, but nothing worked. As the elevator was coming to a stop, Atlas took a step back. He opened a portal at his feet, and carefully reached through it to find something to grab hold of. Once he had a firm grip on the railing beneath the elevator, he let his body hang. He closed the portal just as the elevator sprung open.

"Where is he? They said he'd be in here," one of the soldiers said, stepping inside the elevator.

"Maybe he's in a different elevator," another one suggested.

"That's impossible. This is the one they said he'd be in."

"Well, he's not in here, is he?"

"Thanks, Captain Obvious, I didn't notice."

"Wait, they had Captain Obvious in the realm you were from, too?"

"Oh, shut up, would you? Come on, let's search the rest of the floor. He has to be here somewhere." The two left the elevator.

Atlas, hanging below, knew he couldn't hold on much longer. He had to move before he lost his grip and fell down the elevator shaft. He spotted a ladder just above the floor below him. It led to a small hatch in the wall. Atlas calculated the distance to the ladder and realized he wouldn't be able to build up enough momentum to swing to it. He remembered how, at the paintball park, he'd jumped off the tower and his momentum carried him through the portal and propelled him out the other side.

Atlas searched for locations to place his portals. He spotted a second elevator, adjacent to his, ascending at high speed. He released one hand, pulled out a caster, pointed it at the wall across from the ladder, and pressed the button. He then carefully aimed his other caster at the roof of the elevator that was climbing and opened a second portal.

He holstered the caster and swung back and forth to build up enough energy. He took his last swing and released his grip. He fell down the shaft, toward the roof of the approaching elevator. When he reached the portal, he fell through and was propelled out of the first portal across from the ladder. The momentum from the fall launched him clear across the shaft, and he crashed into the ladder.

Barely able to hold on, Atlas struggled to climb the ladder, but eventually got to the hatch and crawled through it just before the elevator sped past him. He found himself in a familiar place, one with long dark passageways.

Great, I'm back in the service corridors, Atlas thought, pulling out his transponder to check the map. It showed he was indeed in the same passageways he'd used to escape the prison. On the floor above him, was his old cellblock and several others new to him. He scrolled through the map until he found the room labeled Purgatory where Lilou and Nico were held and noticed something peculiar. Two soldiers appeared to be standing guard outside the room. But inside, there was only one other life-frequency, aside from Lilou and Nico's. Atlas had expected the room to be heavily guarded. Perhaps his presence in the building had drawn soldiers away from their posts?

Atlas grew nervous. He knew Allister Craum was somewhere in the building. Lilou had said he was nearby. Still, he had to keep moving. Atlas figured if he could find the maintenance hatch to that room, he could sneak inside, free Lilou and Nico, and use his transponder to make a quick escape.

"Lilou, Nico, are you there?" Atlas said through his voice transponder.

Yes, we are. But you must hurry. We only have ten minutes left, Lilou said.

Atlas, there's someone in the room preparing the reactor now, Nico added.

"Don't worry. I'm on my way."

The only way to reach the room in time was to portal-jump through the passageways, which he did, starting with the first hub in the distance until he was directly below the floor where Lilou and Nico were. He climbed a ladder that led to a small hatch on the ceiling above him. When he reached the top, he used his casters to get through the floor.

Atlas found himself in the corner of an immense hall with two rows of massive rectangular columns rising to a high, half-domed ceiling. The entire room appeared to be constructed of a black marble-like stone. Low ambient lighting along the perimeter walls and soft accent lighting on the interior of the columns illuminated the room. He dashed behind a column and carefully gazed around it. At the center of the room, a man in a white lab coat stood next to what Atlas assumed was the quantum reactor. Thick cables attached to the reactor extended to a stage at the front of the room. Two enormous hollow and grey metallic disks sat on the stage, side by side. Three strange symbols were engraved on them. They looked like the ones on his mother's transponder.

At the back of the stage, a wide monitor displayed the reactor's technical data and information. A countdown clock in the right-hand corner of the screen read five minutes and thirty-five seconds. Atlas assumed this was the time remaining before the reactor was operational. On the left side of the stage, stood a row of prison cells. Lilou and Nico were sitting on the floor of one of them.

Okay, I just need to get past one scientist, he thought.

Just as Atlas was about to open two portals and cause the scientist to fall through the floor, then down through the ceiling as he'd done with the soldiers, the scientist checked something on his handheld device and casually walked out of the hall.

Well, that was easy, Atlas thought. He checked his visor. Seeing no other life-frequencies on his heads-up display, he ran for the stage. He was halfway across the room when he heard Lilou calling him. "Atlas! We're over here!" she shouted.

Moments later, Atlas stood in front of their holding cell and placed both hands on the plexiglass door.

"Wait, how did you get past the guards?" Nico said.

"With these," Atlas replied, showing them his devices. "Dr. Faraday helped me finish my father's transponders, and he created these. They're portal-casters, and they can open a wormhole anywhere, just like Elio described."

"Portal-casters. That's a cool name. Did he come up with that, or did you?" Nico said.

"Atlas, can you please get us out of here?" Lilou cut in urgently.

"Oh, right," Atlas said. "Stand back. I'll cast a portal, and you'll be able to walk through the door." He took a step back before being surprised by a sound from the back of the hall.

Clap, Clap, Clap.

A sinister voice echoed through the hall. "Bravo! You made it right on time."

Atlas turned. Allister Craum strolled out from behind one of the columns, followed by four of his personal guards. They wore white tactical uniforms and thick metallic helmets Atlas had never seen before. Atlas accessed his visor's heads-up display, wondering how he could have missed them. He was shocked to find that Craum and his guards' life-frequencies were nowhere on his map.

"What's wrong, boy? You look like you've seen a ghost," Craum mocked him.

Atlas shook his head in disbelief.

"It's really quite simple," Craum said. "Once I confiscated your siblings' voice transponders and figured out how your father's little invention worked, I developed these helmets that block our life-frequencies. Convenient, yes?" he asked rhetorically, knocking on his helmet with his knuckles.

"Atlas, just go," Lilou said. "Use your transponder and open a wormhole to escape," she whispered through the glass.

Atlas's heart raced. He knew he couldn't leave Lilou and Nico behind, but he also knew that if he tried to turn around and cast a portal, one of Craum's soldiers was sure to stop him. "What are you going to do with us?" Atlas asked, frightened.

"I didn't invent this beautiful machine for nothing," Craum said, raising his hand and motioning to his giant metallic disks. "Luckily for your brother and sister, I can send only one of you in at a time. I guess they'll have to settle for watching you die today." Craum turned to one of his guards. "Prepare our guest for Purgatory," he commanded.

The guard marched on stage, confiscated Atlas's helmet, transponder, and portal-casters, then escorted him to a small ramp in front of one of the metallic disks.

Atlas looked at Lilou and Nico. "I'm sorry. You were right. We should have just gone home."

"Atlas, don't say that. It's our fault," Lilou responded. "We were the ones who got caught."

"Turn on the reactor!" Craum shouted to his guards. They looked at one another in confusion. Craum realized they hadn't been trained in the technology. "Fine, I'll do it myself. Useless fools!" he snarled. He walked over to the reactor, worked the controls, then flipped a switch.

The reactor started to hum as a surge of energy traveled through the cables and up to the hollow disks. Suddenly, two massive pitch-black portal-doors formed within the empty space of the disks, opening a doorway to Purgatory.

Two of the guards stood at the bottom of the ramp behind Atlas, ready to force him into the wormhole.

"Any last words, boy?" Craum asked.

Atlas turned to face Craum. His face was a mixture of sadness and anger. "Yes ... why did you kill her?"

"You fool. Your mother was a traitor, like me. She was just too much of a coward to do what had to be done," he said self-righteously.

"Liar!" Atlas shouted, struggling to break free of the guards and get to Craum.

"You know, it's funny how things worked out. You led me to your father, and now your father has led you to me. Your mother put up more of a fight than both of you," Craum replied cruelly.

As the guards pushed Atlas up the ramp toward Purgatory, an earsplitting explosion rocked the building, causing everyone to fall to the floor. This was followed by the sound of the reactor powering down and every light in the room shutting off.

A voice called over the building's intercom: "All pilots to the flight deck. I repeat. All pilots to the flight deck. We are under attack!"

What's happening? Atlas thought as he lay flat on the ramp.

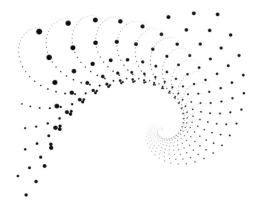

Chapter 21

S till prone, Atlas spotted his portal-casters on the floor in front of him. The shock of the explosion had dislodged them from the guard's belt. Atlas looked at the guard, who was beside him on the floor, and realized he wasn't the only one who had noticed.

He and the guard lunged for the casters at the same time. Luckily, Atlas got to them first. He portal-jumped behind the column on the far-left side of the hall where he'd entered. Although dim emergency lights had come on, the room was still dark, providing Atlas with just enough cover to hide.

"You can't escape from me, Atlas!" Craum shouted.

Atlas ignored him. He stayed hidden with his back against the column, wondering how he'd get out of this. That's when he heard another voice call his name.

Atlas, are you there?

"Mia, is that you? What are you doing here?" Atlas responded in shock, using his internal voice.

We are here to help you, duh!

"What do you mean we? Who else is with you?"

Everyone. The Outliers Alliance from Earth A27. The rebels; they're here!

"Wait, was that explosion yours?"

Yes. Oh, and Frank and Stew are here too. Frank, be quiet, he can't hear you. It doesn't work like that. Sorry Atlas, that was Frank. He says hi.

Atlas glanced out from behind the column to make sure the guards were still on the other side of the hall.

Craum called for him again. "I know you're still in here, Atlas. You wouldn't leave without your little siblings!" he hollered.

Since the guards were still struggling to locate Atlas in the dark, Atlas turned his attention back to Mia. "I don't understand. How did you know I was here?"

The voice transponder. After you sent me to Earth A27, I brought the device to the Outliers Alliance's scientists. They were able to replicate it. Then they used it to track you. As soon as we saw that you'd entered this realm, I told the Outliers Alliance's leaders everything. When they heard your father might be here, they planned this attack.

Atlas was amazed that the rebels had come to his aid. He said, "Mia, meet me on the flight deck in twenty minutes. I have to take care of something."

Atlas, where ... Mia started to say, but he had shut her out of his mind.

Atlas stuck his head out again. Two of Craum's guards were walking through the center of the room, past the reactor. The other two each took one wall, walking on the outside of the columns.

"I know you're back there, Atlas. We will find you!" Craum shouted from the stage.

Atlas remembered what Faraday had told him on the paintball course. He whispered to himself: "Your advantage is not your ability to stay hidden; it's your ability to move."

He took a deep breath and used his portal casters to open a door on the column in front of him, and another on the far-left wall behind the guard coming up the right side. As soon as he stepped through the first door, he snuck up behind the guard, tapped him on his right shoulder, then ran past him to his left. The guard swiveled around to see who had tapped him. By the time he turned back around, Atlas had portal-jumped to the other side of the room, behind the column closest to the stage.

"He's over here!" the guard shouted. The other soldiers turned and pointed their rifles at the right side of the room, where the guard Atlas had tapped was spinning in circles, looking for him.

With all four guards focused on the right side of the room, Atlas repeated his portal-jumping-tapping trick with the guard on the left side of the room before portal-jumping to behind the column furthest from the stage.

"No, he's over here!" the second guard shouted.

"For heaven's sake, he's just a teenager! Find him, you incompetent fools!" Craum yelled from the stage.

All four guards backstepped to the center of the room until their backs were touching. They slowly turned in a circle to prevent Atlas from sneaking up behind them again.

Atlas carefully looked out from behind the column, pointed a caster at the inside of the column closest to the guards, and opened a portal.

One of them spotted it. He shouted, "Look, it's one of his portals!" All four turned and pointed their rifles at the column, waiting for Atlas to emerge.

While they were distracted, Atlas crept to the column on the opposite side and opened a second portal, facing the guards. He stood in front of it and shouted, "I'm right here!"

As the guards turned and fired at him, Atlas jumped through the portal, falling flat on the floor as he emerged on the other side. The energy pulses from the guards' rifles flew across the room, through the column and over Atlas's head. They hit the guards in the back and all four fell to the floor, lifeless.

Atlas picked himself up, holstered his casters, and walked over to the fallen guards. He searched the guards and found his stolen transponder. He picked up one of their rifles and walked to the stage. As he did so, he was almost knocked back down as a second explosion rocked the building.

A voice called over the intercom again. "We have been overrun. All commanding officers retreat to Headquarters. I repeat. We have been overrun. All commanding officers retreat to Headquarters."

As Atlas neared the stage, he was greeted by the sound of Allister Craum clapping his hands once more.

Clap, Clap, Clap.

"I have to say, boy, I was wrong about you. You did put up quite the fight," Craum said, reaching for his transponder.

Atlas fired the rifle twice, hitting Craum with an energy pulse to his arm and leg.

Craum dropped the transponder and fell to his knees. "Good shot. Ugh. I am impressed," he said, grabbing his leg and wincing.

Atlas pointed a caster at Lilou and Nico's cell and created a portal through which they could leave. They ran out to Atlas, who was on the stage, holding his rifle to Craum's chest.

"Atlas, thank heaven you're okay. I couldn't tell what was happening in the dark," Lilou said.

Still holding the rifle on Craum, Atlas said, "Nico, how do we turn this machine back on?"

"Umm ... let me see what I can do. It looks like it lost power during the explosion." Nico went over to the reactor to assess the damage.

"What are you going to do to me now, boy?" Craum asked.

"I'm going to do to you what you did to my father," Atlas replied.

Nico called out, "Atlas, the reactor is still intact. The system just needs to be reset."

"Can you do it?" Atlas called back.

"I can try." Nico bent and opened the reactor's control panel. He located the circuit box and pumped the breakers, then he worked the controls. "There, that should do it. All we need to do now is flip the switch," he said.

"Stand up," Atlas ordered Craum.

"My leg. It's …" Craum began.

"I said, stand up!" Atlas screamed.

Craum slowly got to his feet and stepped up the ramp as Atlas continued to point the rifle at him.

"You know, the reactor has only one charge left. If you send me to Purgatory now, you won't be able to save your father," Craum sneered.

"You're lying," Atlas retorted, sure that Craum was stalling.

"No. It's true. I can bring him back. I just need my transponder. All the data is stored on it. I just have to lock onto him and reopen it while the reactor is on," Craum said, looking down at his transponder on the floor.

Lilou pleaded, "Atlas, don't do it. He's lying. As soon as he has the transponder, he'll try to escape."

"How do I know you're not trying to trick me again?" Atlas asked.

"You don't," Craum replied calmly. "That's the beauty of it," he added, knowing Atlas had no choice but to trust him.

"Lilou, pick up his transponder," Atlas said.

"Altas, you can't …"

"Lilou, please."

She picked up Craum's transponder and tried to turn it on.

"It won't work for you, darling. You have to give it to me," Craum said.

Lilou looked at Atlas for approval before handing it to Craum, who took the transponder and opened a holographic list of names and faces. As he scrolled through the list, Atlas was shocked to see how many people Craum had sent to Purgatory over the years. "Ah, here he is," Craum said, pointing at a picture and name on the display which read "Elio Seeker."

"Seeker ..." Atlas mumbled, realizing he hadn't known his family name.

"Atlas, the reactor is ready, but it no longer has a full charge. Once I turn it on, you'll only have a few seconds to reopen your father's wormhole," Nico said.

"Just do it, Nico," Atlas said, placing his finger on the trigger, ready to react if Craum tried anything funny.

Nico flipped the switch. Once again, the machine hummed as a surge of energy traveled through the cables beneath their feet. Just as before, two black portal-doors appeared on stage.

"Open it!" Atlas shouted at Craum.

Craum stood still, staring at Atlas.

Atlas looked up at the monitor and saw that the reactors charge was quickly draining.

"I said, open it!" Atlas repeated, pushing the rifle into Craum's chest.

Craum shrugged, then calmly selected Elio Seeker's name from the database and released him from Purgatory.

The reactor powered down and caused the emergency lights in the room to flicker.

"What happened? What did you do?" Atlas asked Craum, who stared at Atlas with a look of satisfaction on his face. "Where is he?" Atlas shouted, looking at the disk behind Craum.

"Atlas look!" Lilou said, pointing across the stage. Atlas turned to his right and saw a man on his hands and knees in front of the disk on the other side of the stage.

"Lilou, take this. If Craum moves or opens his mouth, shoot him," Atlas said. He handed her the rifle and ran across the stage.

The closer Atlas got, the less he thought the man looked like his father. When Atlas was standing right above him, the man looked up and said, "Atlas, my child, is that you?"

"Father?" Atlas said, confused. This man was old, probably in his nineties. Then Atlas saw the man's eyes and realized it *was* his father. Although he had been sent to Purgatory only the day before, Elio looked as if he had aged decades.

"Yes, my child, it's me. It's been a long time. I'm sorry. I failed you, and I failed the Rebellion," he said, barely able to speak.

"No, you didn't fail. Remember, back in the cabin, you told me that your mission was to free your home realm. Well, the rebels — the Outliers Alliance they're here. They are freeing your realm right now, as we speak," Atlas said as another explosion rocked the building.

Elio looked up and gave Atlas a small smile, but he didn't respond.

"Father, I need to know something. Allister Craum said my mother was a traitor. Is it true?"

"No Atlas, your mother would never. It took me ages in Purgatory to realize the truth, and that Allister was lying. I believe that after she learned about Allister's plan to defect, she only pretended to join his cause," Elio said, his breath ragged.

"I don't understand. Why would she do that?"

"To protect you, Atlas. She needed to gain Allister's trust so she could access his transponder and delete any trace of the existence of your realm." Elio struggled to speak as he explained his conjecture ...

***

"Elena, we can't stay here, it's not safe," Allister pleaded as he peered through the hotel window that overlooked Boise.

"Elio knows what he's doing," Elena replied, pushing herself up from the couch.

Allister turned and moved toward her. "Elena, you're nine months pregnant," he said. "We can't hide from them anymore. P.O.R.T.A.L. is going to find us. Elio will get us all killed. What are we doing here, anyway? This is a Class B realm. The people here can't help us. They don't have the technology," he said, throwing up his hands.

"You know why we're here, Allister. Elio believes Malcolm Faraday can help us."

"Oh please, Elena. Not this again. I told you; Faraday is just another doppelganger. Do I have to remind you that the last one Elio found was a nutcase?"

"Elio believes Faraday is different — that Faraday can finish his work and save the Rebellion."

"Why? Because some crazy Oracle told him so?" Allister said, shaking his head.

Elena grabbed Allister's arm. "Allister, if you can't trust Elio, then please, trust me."

At the touch of Elena's hand, Allister's demeanor softened. He took her hand in his. "Elena, come with me. I've found a way out."

"What possible way out is there?"

"Just listen. We can't win this war. P.O.R.T.A.L. will always control the Multiverse. They have all the resources and we have so few. The fighting must stop. There's another way to establish peace and allow us to stop hiding."

Elena pulled her hand away and took a step back. "I can't believe what you're saying."

"Listen, I know this is hard to hear, but it must be done. I've made all the arrangements. P.O.R.T.A.L. will let both of us go. We can be free again. Do you remember what it was like to be free?" He looked down at Elena's swollen belly. "Is this the world you want your child to grow up in. A world at constant war?"

Elena put both hands over her stomach, as if to protect her child. "How do you know they won't keep hunting us?"

Allister grabbed a pen and a piece of paper off a small notepad and scribbled something on it. "Because we're going to give them what they want. They don't want us — they want Elio. This note contains the coordinates to this realm and Elio's home realm, where P.O.R.T.A.L has built a new prison. I'll send them this note. They'll find him here, capture him, and send him to Prison, and it will all be over."

Elena turned away and stood beside the couch. Her shoulder bag was on it. She casually took her transponder out of it and draped it around her neck. She faced Allister again. "Really? You want me to give them my husband? After everything he's done for us — for you?"

"What he's done for me? He's brought us into a hell he's created, where we're forced to live in fear, and the only escape is to defeat the most powerful force in the Multiverse!" Allister cried. "I can't accept that anymore." He held out his right hand. "Elena, come with me. I can take care of both of you."

Elena looked down at her belly, her face sad. She pretended to consider Allister's proposal. Finally, she reached out and grabbed his hand, the one containing the note, and pulled it close to her chest. She locked eyes with Allister and nodded her head, implying that she was willing to go along with his plan. She even put her head on his shoulder. After an uncertain moment, he embraced her.

As he did so, Elena cautiously unhooked Allister's transponder from its lanyard and placed it behind her back. Then she gently removed the note from his hand and moved out of his arms.

Allister, overwhelmed with emotion, went back to the window to gather his thoughts. "Elena, I always knew it. I knew you would come with me."

While he was distracted, Elena placed the note in her pocket and entered a kill-command into his transponder, deleting every coordinate stored in its memory. Then she turned on her own device.

Allister reached for his transponder for reassurance. Finding it missing, he looked and saw Elena entering a coordinate into her transponder.

"What are you doing?" He lunged for her device, trying to dislodge it. She struggled against him and managed to enter the last number of the coordinate. Instantly, a portal appeared behind Allister. Unaware of this, he saw his own transponder in Elena's other hand and snatched it from her.

He smirked. "What were you planning on doing with this, anyway?" Pulling his eyes away for a moment, he saw the portal behind him.

Without hesitation, Elena pushed Allister into the opening. But as she tried to close the wormhole, something seized her legs and she fell to the floor. Behind her, Allister's hands protruded from the portal. He gripped her legs and tried to pull her into it with him. Although she kicked with all her might, he drew her closer and turned her over, so she was lying face up. Then he hauled himself out of the wormhole and gripped her tightly around the neck in frustration and anger. Elena kicked and fought and gasped for air. But with each passing moment, she grew weaker, until her life drained away.

Allister stood and looked down in shock at what he'd done. Then, he heard a key turning in the lock. Panicked, Alister left Elena's body where it lay and vanished into the wormhole.

As the hotel door swung open, Elena's lifeless hand fell on top of her transponder, closing the wormhole, and erasing all evidence of what had occurred.

"Elena! Allister! I found him!" Elio shouted. "I disguised myself and convinced him to move to Stanford to begin his research." He shut the door behind him and walked into the small living area. "Elena ... Elena!"

***

"It's the only explanation for why Allister never went back, or why P.O.R.T.A.L. hasn't taken control of your realm. It's because they don't know it exists." Elio reached up, clutched Atlas's shoulder, and pulled him closer. "Atlas, listen to me. You must keep it that way. Don't make the same mistakes I did. Your realm can never know the existence of the Multiverse," he said before releasing his grip.

Just then, the front door to the hall blew open, and a small squadron of soldiers rushed in.

Atlas, Lilou, and Nico turned to see what had happened. While their backs were to him, Craum snatched the transponder from Lilou's hand, opened a wormhole and escaped.

"Atlas, he's gone!" Lilou shouted.

Atlas saw that Craum had indeed vanished. He looked back at the entrance to the hall. Mia was running toward them behind a squadron of rebel soldiers.

"Atlas!" she called out, racing past the reactor and up the stage. She couldn't see Elio as Atlas was blocking her view.

"Mia, you found us." Atlas felt torn between his excitement at seeing his friend again and his conversation with his father.

"We couldn't find you on the flight deck, so we tracked your life-frequency to this room," Mia explained. "The rebels have taken control of the entire building. They're freeing the prisoners from the cells now," she added.

"Atlas, look!" Lilou shouted, pointing at Elio. Atlas's father lay on the ramp, unmoving.

"Father!" Atlas cried out. "Quick, somebody help him!"

A rebel soldier rushed up, knelt beside Elio, and checked his pulse. He looked at Atlas and shook his head.

"He's gone," Atlas said. Although Atlas had seen Elio struggling to hold himself up and speak, he hadn't expected his father to die so quickly.

Lilou ran across the stage and hugged Atlas. "I'm so, so sorry. It all happened so fast," she said.

"It's okay," Atlas said. *It's okay,* he told himself, finding comfort in the fact that he'd gotten the resolution he needed.

The soldier who had checked Elio's body said, "Son, if you don't mind, we're going to take your father's body to one of the transports now."

Atlas nodded and watched the rebel soldiers pick up Elio's body to carry it to the flight deck.

"What did he say to you?" Lilou asked.

"He said my mother is the reason P.O.R.T.A.L. never discovered our realm and that she sacrificed herself to keep me safe ... to keep *us* safe," Atlas told Mia, Lilou, and Nico.

Mia, watching Elio's body being carried away, noticed how much he had aged. "I don't understand. What happened to him?"

"Allister Craum sent him to Purgatory. We used the reactor's remaining charge to free him, but it was too late," Atlas said, catching a last glimpse of his father.

"But *when?*" Mia said. "When did he send your father to Purgatory?"

"Yesterday."

"Yesterday? He'd only been in there a day?" Mia asked quietly, staring at the ground where Elio's body had been.

"Yes. Somehow, Purgatory aged him. It's like he was in there for decades."

Mia looked frightened. "My mother, if she was sent there years ago, do you think that means she's ..."

"Dead?" Nico interrupted. "No, if your mother was sent to Purgatory, she's not dead."

Lilou looked startled. "Nico, why would you say that? You saw what happened to Atlas's father."

"Yes, but I also saw the list of names on Craum's transponder. If Purgatory aged you until you died, there wouldn't be any names left on that list."

"He's right," Atlas said. "Craum said he wanted Elio to spend an eternity in Purgatory."

"What does that mean? Is my mother still alive?" Mia asked.

Nico answered her. "I don't exactly know how it works, but time seems to work differently inside Purgatory," he said.

Atlas turned to his brother. "Nico, you said the reactor could slow down time. Can it reverse time too?"

"Theoretically, yes. But we used the reactor's last charge to free your father. We'd need an alternative energy source, and one powerful enough to keep Purgatory open for longer," Nico answered. He paced the stage, thinking.

"An energy source like Element X?" Atlas said, raising an eyebrow.

Nico's eyes widened. "You found it, didn't you? I knew it."

"Yes. It's what powers my new transponder."

"Wait, how did you find it?" Mia said. "I was there. We didn't leave the mines with Element X."

"Yes, we did. We got covered in it when we fell down that mineshaft," Atlas explained.

Lilou brought up a critical detail. "Nico, what about the transponder with the list of names?" she said. "Craum took it with him when he escaped."

"Hmm. We may not be able to select who we release, but if Element X can flood the reactor with enough energy, it might be strong enough to release everyone at once," Nico said.

Mia, her heart racing, asked, "My mother, will she be like how I remember her?"

"I can't promise anyone will be the same age they were when they went in," Nico replied. "But slowing time and reversing time are two sides of the same coin. We need to keep the reactor on, and Purgatory open for as long as we can. The longer the doors are open, the more time will be reversed."

"But what if it doesn't work?" Mia asked.

"We have to try," Atlas said, pulling out his father's transponder. He took one last look at it, lifted it above his head, and hurled it to the floor, shattering it. He reached down, removed its fuel cell and tossed it to Nico. "Here, take this. Inside, you'll find Element X."

Nico opened the reactor's control panel and removed its spent fuel cell. Then he carefully cracked open the transponder's fuel cell containing Element X, injected the element into the reactor's fuel cell, and pushed that cell back into place. The monitor showed that the reactor was now fully charged.

"There, it's ready," Nico said.

"I hope this works," Mia added.

"It will," Atlas assured her. "Nico, turn it back on."

Nico worked the controls, flipped the switch, and the reactor came back to life. This time, a surge of energy even bigger than before forced Nico to step back from the reactor, which shook as if it might explode. On the stage, the two portal-doors reopened. Flashes of electricity caused by charged particles in the air lit up the stage.

"Nothing's happening!" Mia shouted over the sound of the reactor, staring intently at the portal-doors.

Atlas looked at the monitor and yelled, "Nico! The charge is draining fast!"

"Just wait!" Nico yelled back. "We need to keep it open a little longer."

After a full minute, the flashes of electricity subsided, and the reactor fell silent.

All at once, a stream of people began to emerge from the portal-doors. They all looked confused, as they tried to figure out what was happening and where they were.

Atlas, Lilou, Nico, and Mia found themselves surrounded by a sea of people. Those on stage had to move into the hall to make room as more and more people exited the portals.

Mia scanned the crowd for her mother. "Kyla!" she cried out, hoping her mom would hear her name above the commotion. "Kyla!"

"Mia-Mia, is that you?" a voice called back.

"Mom!" Mia yelled as she spotted her mother on stage, walking down the ramp Elio had come out of. Mia forced her way through the crowd and back on stage to hug her mother.

The rebel soldiers who'd had carried Elio to the flight deck returned to the hall. They stared at the crowd, perplexed. One took out his radio device, and said, "Sir, we're going to need more transports — a lot more."

Eventually, the progression of people streaming out of portal-doors slowed. When the last prisoner left Purgatory, the reactor ran out of energy and shut down.

At the center of the hall, Atlas, Lilou, and Nico directed the freed prisoners toward the soldiers at the back.

"There must be close to a hundred people in here," Lilou said.

"You did it, Nico!" Atlas exclaimed.

"*We* did it," Nico replied.

Mia and a woman who appeared in her mid-thirties, with ebony skin, black hair, and a wide smile came up to the siblings. "Atlas, I want you to meet someone. This is my mom, Kyla," Mia said, holding her mom's hand tightly.

Kyla gave each of the siblings a hug. "Thank you all so much," she said. "I'm so grateful to be free and to have my daughter back. How can I ever repay you?"

"You don't have to. I'm happy we weren't too late," Atlas replied.

Mia said, "I'll meet you guys on the flight deck. Frank and Stew are waiting for us there."

Atlas grinned and waved to Mia and her mom as they walked away.

When everyone had gone, Atlas and his siblings remained behind for a moment. Lilou said, "Atlas, your portal-casters, do they still work?"

"No. Not without my transponder and not without Element X. It's okay. I don't need them anymore." He tossed them on the floor. "Come on. It's time for us to go home."

At the flight deck, squadrons of rebel soldiers were guiding the freed prisoners onto transports to take them to Earth A27.

They boarded Mia's ship with Frank, Stew, and Mia's mother. When the ship was far enough away from the city, Frank opened a portal in the sky with the craft's onboard transponder. Just before they entered it, Atlas took one last look at Earth A14, the realm where his mother and father had been born, and the realm his father ultimately helped set free.

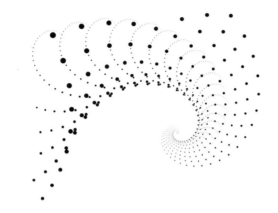

Chapter 22

Mia's ship emerged from the wormhole high above a massive city, one many times larger than the one on Earth A14. It extended as far as the eye could see. Although the city was huge, its buildings were strategically low to the ground. Airships patrolled the sky, and hundreds of defensive towers with enormous guns pointed skyward.

The city looked like a giant military base. The buildings were made of a matte-black metallic material, giving the impression that they were heavily armored.

Atlas peered down at it through his window. "Where are we?" he asked Mia, who was piloting the ship.

"This is Earth A27, the Outliers Alliance Headquarters."

"I don't understand. This is bigger than P.O.R.T.A.L.'s headquarters."

Frank, who was working the craft's control panel, burst out laughing.

"What's so funny?" Atlas asked.

Nico answered for Frank. "I think he means the building you were in wasn't P.O.R.T.A.L.'s headquarters," he said.

Frank looked over his shoulder to see who was speaking. He said, "Your brother's very smart. He's right. That building was a Central Hub, or better yet, just an outpost. P.O.R.T.A.L.'s headquarters is Earth A1."

"You mean it's *on* Earth A1?" Atlas said.

Stew put in, "No, he means their headquarters is Earth A1. It's a military base the size of an entire planet."

"Hey, don't get me wrong," Frank said. "You did a noble thing today. That was an important hub, and you saved a lot of lives. And if we can reinstate the local government, we'll have another strategically in this war."

"What do you mean, *we?* I thought you were a smuggler," Atlas said.

"Not anymore. Stew and I spent two long years in that prison. After you and your father freed us, we joined the Alliance," Frank said, proudly displaying his armband with the Outliers Alliance emblem. It depicted an image of five earths in the shape of a star, with the letters OA at its center.

"What about you?" Atlas asked Mia, not seeing the same band on her arm.

"I haven't decided," Mia said. "Right now, all I can think about is spending time with my mom." She glanced over her shoulder at her mother, who was sitting in the ship's small cargo hold.

As they neared the ground, Mia steered the craft alongside several others and hovered above a large circular door built into the ground, waiting for clearance. When the door opened, she and the other pilots lowered their crafts into an underground hangar.

"Where are you taking us now?" Lilou asked when they disembarked.

"General Armstrong requested that I bring you all in to be debriefed. After that, it's up to you."

Atlas saw rebel soldiers placing Elio's body on a gurney. "What will happen to my father?" he asked.

"I don't know yet," Mia replied.

She directed her mom to a medic's station to be checked out. Then she guided Atlas, Lilou, and Nico to an office in an underground bunker. "General Armstrong is through that door. I'm going to leave you guys here. Atlas, will you call me on a voice transponder when you're done?"

"Of course."

The siblings eyed the solid metal door, wondering what to do next. After several seconds, Lilou said, "Are we supposed to knock?"

"I'm not going to knock," Atlas said anxiously.

Lilou giggled. "You just broke into a P.O.R.T.A.L. Central Hub, freed hundreds of prisoners, and now you're too scared to knock?"

"Well, if you're so brave, why don't you knock?"

"Because I don't want to," she said.

"I find it strange that we should have to knock at all, considering they know we're standing out here," Nico said, pointing to a camera above the door.

"Okay. How about Rock, Paper, Scissors?" Atlas suggested.

Lilou said, "Okay, fine. Ready: Rock, Paper, Sciss-"

Just then, the door swung open, and a man in a military uniform greeted them. "What are you kids doing?"

"Umm ... we're sorry. We didn't know if we were supposed to knock," Atlas answered, looking down at the floor.

"No, you're not supposed to knock. You're supposed to buzz us," the soldier said, pointing to the buzzer on the wall next to the door. "Forget it. Just come inside."

They found themselves in a small, dark office. The walls were bare, and the room was almost empty, with only a small table displaying a holographic map of the Multiverse, and an oversize desk at the back.

"Are you General Armstrong?" Atlas asked.

"No, that's General Armstrong," the man said, motioning to a man sitting behind the desk. Armstrong was facing away from them.

"Atlas, Nico, Lilou, come on in. Don't be scared," the man said, spinning around.

The soldier left, and the siblings walked over to the desk. Atlas stopped to take a closer look at the holographic map. He could almost make out the movement of rebel troops. General Armstrong, a tall man in his fifties with dark skin and receding grey hair, stood and walked around the desk to greet them.

"Ah, I see you noticed my map. P.O.R.T.A.L. is not the only organization in the Multiverse with advanced technology. I can track the movement of all the rebel troops right here from this room. As you can see, our troops have launched a full-scale invasion of Earth A14. It will be the first realm we have conquered in the past twelve years.

"But enough about that. I'm thrilled to meet our three heroes. I've heard so much about you all," Armstrong said, shaking each of their hands. As he shook Nico's hand, he said, "Nico, the hero who freed the prisoners from Purgatory." He turned to Lilou. "And Lilou. Is it true you released an angry herd of triceratops into P.O.R.T.A.L.'s barracks?"

"I did do that, didn't I?" she said proudly.

"And finally, Atlas, son of Elio. The boy who found the lost father of the Rebellion and broke into one of the most secure hubs in the Multiverse and rescued thousands. I can't wait to hear the whole story."

"But sir, my father didn't make it, and Allister Craum got away," Atlas said, not feeling much like a hero.

"I know, son. I'm sorry to hear about your father. We all are. But you have to understand, after word got out that your father was alive, there was a spark in the Rebellion. I've had more soldiers enlist in the last week than in the twelve years since Elio disappeared. Freeing Earth A14 is just the beginning. As for Allister Craum, don't worry about that low-level scum. His failures will not go unnoticed by the Council."

"Sir, do you know who the Council is? My friend Mia told me that nobody knows. Is that true?" Atlas asked.

The general paused. Atlas tried to read his expression, but he couldn't tell if Armstrong's hesitation was because he didn't know the answer, or because he didn't want to share it.

"Look, all you need to know is that the Council is evil. And until that evil stops spreading, the Multiverse will never be free. Now, I don't know exactly what your situation is, but the Rebellion could really use heroes like yourselves," the general said.

Atlas looked at his brother and sister, then back at Armstrong. "I promised my mother that all three of us would come home. I have to keep that promise."

Armstrong placed his hand on Atlas's shoulder. "I understand. You know what? We can debrief tomorrow. Why don't you three get some rest tonight? Tomorrow there will be a funeral for a hero, and then we will get you home. You have my word."

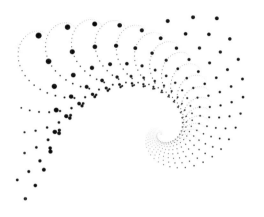

Chapter 23

"Nico, come on! We're going to be late!" Lilou shouted, putting on a pair of dress shoes, part of the outfit she'd been given by the Outliers Alliance.

Nico was also wearing new clothes from the Alliance. "This suit doesn't fit. I think it's too small," Nico said, trying to straighten his collar.

Lilou sounded annoyed. "I think it's supposed to look like that. Who cares? The ceremony will start in fifteen minutes."

"I thought it was a funeral?"

"It is, but they're also celebrating their victory on Earth A14." Lilou held open the door to their room in the underground barracks.

"Where's Atlas?" Nico asked, walking past her into the hallway.

"He left early this morning. He had to speak with General Armstrong, then he wanted to hang out with Mia. She was helping him with his speech. He'll meet us at the funeral," Lilou said.

"You mean the ceremony?" Nico corrected her.

"Yeah, whatever. Let me see if I can get a hold of him," Lilou said, pressing the button on her voice transponder. "Atlas, are you there?"

I'm here. Where are you guys? Everyone else is already here, Atlas said.

Lilou rolled her eyes. "Sorry, you can blame Nico for that. We're on our way now. Where are we supposed to go?"

Just follow the crowd to the stadium and look for me on stage. There are two seats for you next to me and Mia.

"Wait, we're going to be on stage?"

Yeah, and I hope you guys are ready because there are quite a few people here, he said nervously.

Once outside, Lilou and Nico followed a huge crowd to the stadium, which was filled with thousands of people. In front of the enormous stage, several rebel soldiers guarded Elio's body as it lay in an open casket on a raised platform. A row of officers in dress uniforms sat on the left-hand side of the stage, including General Armstrong. On the right-hand side, Atlas and Mia occupied two of four seats.

"Those two empty seats must be for us," Nico whispered.

"Let's hurry. It looks like it's about to start."

As they got to their seats, the crowd stood. Each person placed their right hand over their chest with their fingers spread, symbolizing the five original realms that made up the Outliers Alliance. A live band played what the siblings assumed was the Outliers Alliance anthem. As the last notes sounded, a woman's voice came over the stadium's P.A. system. "Please remain standing for President Xavier."

A man in a fancy blue suit walked on stage and up to the podium. He nodded, indicating that everyone should retake their seats.

Leaning across Nico and Mia, Lilou whispered to Atlas, "That's the president? He looks young."

Mia, the only one who knew anything about the Outliers Alliance, whispered back, "Yeah, and inexperienced too. There are a lot of people who don't like him, including me."

President Xavier looked right at them, as if he could hear them. Then he turned toward the crowd. "We are gathered here today to honor a hero and celebrate our victory over P.O.R.T.A.L. and the Council. I was twenty-three when Elio Seeker disappeared. Back then, he was regarded as a symbol of truth and justice in the Multiverse, and many perceived him to be our savior, the person who would bring about an end to this war. But we were wrong. Elio is not just a symbol of truth and justice; he's also a symbol of hope and sacrifice.

"If we've learned anything from his twelve years in exile, it's that no single individual can win this war. It's a collective effort, one that requires both hope and sacrifice from everyone. To remind us of Elio's sacrifice, we have erected a statue in his honor." The president faced a curtain at the back of the stage. It dropped, revealing a giant bronze statue of a young Elio.

The crowd stood and cheered.

Lilou leaned over again and said, "It looks a lot like Dr. Faraday."

"It does. That's what my father looks like without his beard," Atlas replied.

Several more speeches from the top generals followed. General Armstrong went last and spoke about their victory on Earth A14. Atlas, however, wasn't listening; he was wiping the sweat from his hands and reviewing the notes he and Mia had put together earlier that morning.

Armstrong finished his speech by briefly talking about the individual triumphs of Mia, Lilou, and Nico. Last, he shared some of Atlas's exploits. He turned to Atlas. "Now," he said, "please welcome a special guest, Atlas Seeker, son of Elio Seeker." Armstrong clapped his hands along with the crowd.

Atlas, surprised at hearing himself called by his family name, found himself rooted to his seat.

Mia nudged him. "Atlas, you're supposed to go up."

Returning to reality, Atlas walked to the podium. He reached into his pockets for his notes and realized he'd left them beneath his chair. He froze for a second, then sighed. Realizing it was too late to go back for them, he began.

"Hi, my name is Atlas," he said, followed by an awkward pause. As he struggled to think of what to say, he spotted Kyla, Esme and her children, Frank and Stew, and many of the other prisoners he'd helped to free sitting in the front row. Seeing them, a flood of memories from the past few weeks came rushing back, providing him with the inspiration he needed. "Five weeks ago, I didn't know that the Multiverse existed. The only thing I had to worry about was making it through a day in middle school without the school bully noticing me. I realize now that I was scared of the school bully for the same reason that I wanted to find my father — I didn't know who I was, or where I came from. Growing up as an orphan, never knowing who my birth mother and father were, made me feel isolated and alone.

"But after everything I've been through, I realize that I'm not alone. In fact, I've never been alone. I have a mother who cares for me deeply, a sister who is always looking out for me, a brother who can solve any problem, and now I have something I've never had before — a friend," Atlas said, looking at Mia.

"President Xavier is wrong," he said. A sea of puzzled faces looked back at him. "It takes more than hope and sacrifice to make a change. It takes courage. Hope takes courage. Sacrifice takes courage. And it takes courage to pick ourselves back up when we fall — because sometimes we do fall, and sometimes we do fail. My father once told a professor I know that 'The courage of the few, decide the fate of the many.' I didn't get a chance to ask my father what he meant by that. But I think he meant that if we have courage, then we have the power to control our destiny."

***

When the siblings returned to their rooms, their backpacks and outfits from home lay on each of their beds.

"Where did these come from?" Atlas asked.

"The rebels must have recovered them from the Hub," Nico guessed. He opened his backpack. "Look, Dr. Faraday's book is still in here."

All three changed out of the formal clothes they'd been given and put on their school clothes.

Atlas stuffed Faraday's suit into his backpack. "I guess that's it," he said, throwing his backpack over his shoulder.

"How are we getting home?" Lilou asked.

"Mia says she wants to open the wormhole for us so we can say goodbye to her," Atlas said.

They walked down the hall to Mia's room.

"Perfect timing, my mother just left," she said, opening the door. "I can't thank you guys enough. My mother is so happy and grateful to be home, and I'm thrilled to have her back."

"I'm just glad it all worked out, and we were able to free everyone from Purgatory," Atlas replied.

There was an awkward pause. None of them knew how to say goodbye.

Lilou broke the silence. "So, what will you do now?" she asked Mia.

"I don't know. My mother and I will stay here a while since we don't have anywhere else to go. General Armstrong said we could stay as long as we need to, but I'm hoping that someday we can return to our home realm and start over." Mia looked at Atlas. "What about you guys? Have any of you thought about staying here and joining the Rebellion?"

"I'm sorry, but we can't," Atlas said. "I promised our mother we'd come home."

"I totally understand. She'll be really glad to see you — and relieved." Mia picked up the transponder the Outliers Alliance had given her. "Well, I guess it's time to get you home," she said. "Wait ... How do we get you home? Your realm isn't programmed into my transponder. Do any of you know the coordinates?"

The three looked at each other, mystified. Then, Atlas smiled. "The note!" he exclaimed, reaching into his back pocket. "It's still here," he added, relieved.

"The note from the box?" Lilou said.

"Yes. When I opened the first wormhole, I entered the first set of numbers. The second set of numbers must be to take us back home." Atlas handed the note to Mia.

"How do we know it will take you home and not to some other realm?" she asked.

"It came from our realm. Whoever wrote that note must have written down the return coordinates," Atlas said. "It will work. I know it will."

"Okay. I'll give it a try." Mia typed the series of numbers into the transponder's interface.

Two points on the hologram lit up, and a pathway between them formed. The pathway changed to a bright light as the space in front of them tore open, revealing an iridescent portal.

"I guess this is goodbye then," Atlas said, his voice tight.

"Atlas wait. Take this." Mia reached under her bed and pulled out a box. "But don't open it until you get home."

Atlas grabbed the box from Mia. Although he was eager to find out what was inside, he replied, "I won't. I promise."

"After this, I'll have your realm's coordinates stored on my transponder, so don't be surprised if I show up out of the blue," Mia said, smiling.

Atlas returned the smile. "I don't think I would mind at all," he said.

Holding hands, Atlas, Lilou, and Nico said their last goodbyes and stepped into the light.

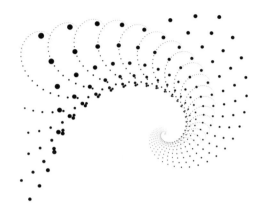

Chapter 24

The siblings materialized on the fifty-yard line at Albertsons Stadium on the Boise State campus. Luckily, the stadium was empty, so no one saw them or the portal. They hurried to the stadium's exit.

The campus outside was crowded with students; it must have been the middle of the week, with fall classes in full swing.

"If we start now, we can be home in thirty minutes," Lilou said.

"Wait ... we're close to Dr. Faraday's lab," Atlas said. "I need to let him know we're back. And we need to figure out what we're going to tell Adora," he added.

Lilou thought about this. "Okay, fine," she said. "We see Dr. Faraday, come up with a story, and then go home."

"Atlas, don't you want to know what's in the box Mia gave you?" Nico asked.

"I don't want to open it here. Let's wait until we're alone somewhere."

Atlas led the way to the science building and down to the lab. He peeked through the blinds on the door. Not seeing Faraday, he knocked.

They waited, but nobody answered.

"Check and see if the door is unlocked," Lilou suggested.

Atlas turned the handle, cautiously pushed the door open, and went in. Faraday was sitting at the far end of the lab working at a small welding station. He was wearing headphones and goggles, and his back was to them.

"Dr. Faraday!" Atlas called out. "Dr. Faraday! I'm back!"

"He can't hear you," Lilou said.

They walked over and stood behind him. "Malcolm!" Atlas shouted.

Startled, Faraday dropped his welding tool and whipped his head around. "Atlas, you scared the bejesus out of me!" he exclaimed, removing his headphones and goggles. "Wait — you're back! And your brother and sister are back too. You did it, didn't you!" He stood and hugged Atlas.

"Yes, we're back. For good this time," Atlas said.

"What about your father?"

Atlas shook his head.

"I'm really sorry, kid."

"It's okay. He told me what I needed to know. I'm just happy we're home and that Lilou and Nico are safe."

"Where are your portal-casters?" Faraday said, seeing that Atlas was no longer wearing his special suit.

"They didn't make it back," Atlas replied sadly. "We had to use the remaining Element X from the transponder to free all the prisoners from Purgatory. Now we have no way of returning to the Multiverse."

Faraday smiled. "That might not be entirely true. When I rebuilt your father's transponder, I stored all the software on the quantum computer and took 3-D scans of the parts. I'm trying to build a new model right now. The only thing I'm missing is a power source."

Atlas frowned. "Malcolm," he said, "I made a promise to my father to keep our realm safe. If our realm discovers interdimensional travel, we could be in grave danger."

"What if we don't share the technology with anyone else?" Nico said.

"What do you mean?" Atlas asked him.

"I'm just saying, we, and your father, have traveled through multiple wormholes to and from this realm. As long as we keep it a secret and keep the technology out of the of the government's hands, there should be no way for P.O.R.T.A.L. to track us. Hypothetically, someday, they may discover our realm using their advanced algorithm system. However, with billions of Earths in the Multiverse, the chance is still low."

"You're right. If we realm-hop, P.O.R.T.A.L. won't be able to track us," Atlas said, thinking that he'd like to visit Mia from time to time. "Malcolm, can you promise never to share this technology with anyone? Nobody can know it exists. If it gets into the wrong hands, it could put everyone in this realm in danger."

"I promise, kid. I wouldn't have this technology without you. I owe you that. But like I said, I haven't found a power source. Even typical radioactive materials aren't exactly easy to come by." There was a pause in the conversation. Faraday glanced down at what Atlas was holding. "So, what's in the box, kid?"

"Oh, right. I guess it's okay for me to open it now," Atlas said. He turned away from the others and put the box on the table in the center of the room.

He carefully lifted the lid and peered inside. Atlas's eyes lit up. "Mia, you're a genius!" he said. He turned around and held something up for everyone to see.

Lilou clapped her hands. "Is that what I think it is?" she said.

"Yup. It's the clothing Mia wore inside the mines." Lilou began, "But that would mean …"

Nico finished her thought. "It's covered in Element X!"

"This is great! It's exactly what I need to finish the replica of your father's transponder," Faraday exclaimed. "Atlas, can you leave it here in the lab with me?"

"I don't see why not. I have no use for it. Mia must have given it to me for this very reason."

"Atlas, I promise to keep it safe," Faraday assured him. "Now," he said, "We need to get you guys home. Your faces have been all over the news. That detective won't stop calling me."

"What are we supposed to tell our mom?" Atlas said, realizing they hadn't come up with a story.

"She's your mother; you need to tell her the truth. Except I wouldn't tell her about the doppelganger situation; that might freak her out. And as for the media ... you'll need to come up with a story — and a good one."

"What if she doesn't believe us?" Lilou said.

"Oh, I'm fairly certain she won't believe you; at least, not right away. But if you three stick together and keep your story straight, she'll come around. Hey, look at me. I eventually believed you, right?" Faraday said.

"I guess you're right," Atlas replied.

"I tell you what; I'll drive you guys home."

"What about my bike?" Atlas asked, remembering he had left it on campus.

"Don't worry about it. I'm pretty sure Detective Brown took it, anyway. Come on, follow me."

Before they left, Nico pulled out the professor's book. "Did you want this back?" he asked.

"You can keep it. It's outdated now," Faraday said. "And I guess that means I'll need help writing a new one," he added, giving Nico a wink.

They all hopped into Faraday's car, and he drove them across town to the North End. When they arrived at the house, Faraday walked them to the front door. Without knocking, Atlas opened the door, and they all went inside.

Hearing people enter the house unannounced, Adora flew out of the kitchen. Seeing her children, she exclaimed, "You're home! You're all home! Thank heavens you're back." She gave each of them a huge hug. "Who is this?" she said, looking at the professor.

"Ma'am, my name is Malcolm Faraday."

"You, you did this! What did you do to my children?" Adora cried. She picked up a boot lying by the door and raised it over her head.

Atlas jumped in front of Faraday. "Mom, no, he didn't do anything. In fact, he's the reason we came back alive," Atlas said.

Adora crossed her arms over her chest. The boot remained in one hand. "Came back from where? Where have you kids been all this time?"

"Listen, Mom, I wasn't totally honest with you before, but I'm ready to tell the truth now," Atlas said. "We're *all* ready to tell the truth," he added, looking at Lilou and Nico.

"Well, let's hear it then," Adora said. "Let's sit in the dining room. Oh, and you," she said, putting down the boot and pointing a finger at Faraday, "you stay right there; don't go anywhere or I'll call the police."

Faraday stayed in the foyer as the kids followed Adora to the dining room. He heard them tell Adora the entire story, from beginning to end, including parts he was unaware of. After thirty minutes of standing, he decided it would be okay to take a seat on one of the small sofas in the living room.

After what felt like another hour, Atlas, Lilou, Nico, and Adora emerged from the dining room.

"Is it true?" Adora asked Faraday, who jumped up from the couch at the sight of them.

"Yes, it's true," he replied. "As hard as it may be to believe right now, everything they told you is the truth. Your children love you; they wouldn't lie to you about something like this."

Adora wiped tears from her eyes and sighed. "What are we supposed to tell the media?" she asked.

Lilou cleared her throat. "We tell everyone that we ran away. We say we were being bullied at school, so we tried to get back to San Diego."

"Will that work?" Adora said dubiously.

"If we do it as a family, it will work," Atlas replied.

"Okay," Adora said, straightening her back. "You all must be starving. Go back into the dining room, and I'll make dinner."

The siblings turned to walk away, and Faraday headed toward the door.

Adora stopped him. "Aren't you going to stay for dinner?"

He beamed and followed the kids into the dining room. As Adora cooked, Atlas, Lilou, Nico, and the professor swapped stories. Adora returned with the siblings' favorite spaghetti and meatballs. As they ate, the kids talked about how they would handle returning to school.

Meanwhile, Adora and Faraday got to know each other. The siblings couldn't help but notice that Adora frequently broke out in laughter.

"Have either of you ever seen Mom laugh so hard?" Lilou whispered, looking across the table at the adults.

"Not that I can remember," Atlas replied.

"I don't recall Dr. Faraday being very funny," Nico added.

Atlas grinned. "Me neither, but Mom sure seems to think he is."

When Adora collected the empty plates, Atlas followed her into the kitchen. "Your friend Malcolm is quite the character," she said with a broad smile.

"Yeah, he's great. Isn't he? Say, Mom, I wanted to ask you something."

"Sure, what is it?" Adora replied, giving Atlas her full attention.

"Can you tell me about my adoption?"

"Of course. What do you want to know?"

"Why me? Why would you choose me?"

"Well, as you know, I couldn't have children of my own. But I always knew I wanted to be a mother, so I adopted your brother and sister. I thought that would be it, but a few years later, the adoption agency reached out and asked if I wanted to adopt another child. They sent me a picture of you, and it was strange. I can't explain it, but it felt like I knew you. As soon as I saw you, I felt I was destined to be your mother."

"You don't need to explain. I understand now," Atlas said, feeling a new sense of connection to Adora.

"Wait, I just remembered. I have something for you!" Adora exclaimed. She opened the fridge. "Call me crazy, but I made this for you, even though you were gone," she said, pulling out a birthday cake.

"You did that for me?" Atlas said with a big grin.

"Of course, I wouldn't miss your thirteenth birthday for the world," Adora replied. "Now, come on, grab some plates. Let's go back in there and celebrate."

About the Author

Chandon Siman grew up in California and attended Cal State University of Fullerton. In 2016, he moved with his wife and their two children to Idaho, where he currently teaches Language Arts to middle and upper grades. A fan of Young Adult literature and Science Fiction, he has taken his passion and expertise out of the classroom to produce his first novel, Atlas and the Multiverse: Seeking Courage. Chandon wrote this novel during the pandemic; a story inspired by his children, and the books and movies he grew up on. Chandon plans to expand the world he has created with a series of books based on the same characters.

Made in the USA
Thornton, CO
04/23/24 21:33:41

0069879e-0a37-4ed6-9f67-be88fa5df8f0R01